# AMATEUR Angel

A Lighthearted Metaphysical Novel

Jerry Whitney

Paperback ISBN: 9798333114860

Cover Design: Timothy Kendall

*To my daughter, Dana Marie Whitney, who read and reread these chapters with me. Her helpful suggestions and punctuation corrections, along with Billy Yates, my son-in-law's home-cooked dinners kept me going over the four years it took me to write this book. Much love to you both.*

# PART 1

# Chapter 1

"Ruby Louise Holliday, you are the winner of the tenth annual Metaphysical Lottery." The voice boomed out of the crackly, too-loud sound system.

Ruby looked around the movie theater, filled with giggly teens, more interested in themselves than the squat man standing on the stage. He wore a top hat, yellow and black checkered clown pants, and suspenders that flashed red trickle lights.

"Ruby Louise Holliday, please come to the stage to accept your prize."

She looked down and saw she was wearing her old faded blue swimsuit. She'd thrown it out last summer when the elastic in the legs gave up.

"Ruby Louise, we know you're here. You have the winning ticket."

She stood, holding a family-size popcorn tub in her right arm and a strawberry slush in her left hand.

"Can you come up here?" she called. "I'm loaded *down* . . . and I'm not dressed." Laughter.

"Our *winner* of the tenth annual Metaphysical Lottery is loaded and she's not dressed. Should I go up or should she come down?"

"Down! Down!" the audience chanted.

"Cruel-hearted teens," she muttered. *Oh well, I'll never see these people again.*

Ruby set the tub of popcorn on her seat and positioned her strawberry slush into the cup holder, fully aware that her butt was hanging out of the swimsuit that had surrendered its integrity long ago.

"Scuse me, scuse me, scuse me." She sidled down the row to the aisle, glided down the carpeted steps, and in one leap, cleared the last stair and landed barefoot on the stage. She didn't bother to pull down the back of the swimsuit.

The audience, becoming allies, cheered and clapped.

Ruby Louise strolled over to the announcer, who looked like the man behind the curtain in *The Wizard of Oz*.

"Very well, my dear," he said, stroking his handlebar mustache. "As I said, you have the winning ticket, drawn on this very stage, for the tenth annual Metaphysical Lottery."

"Excuse me, but what *is* a Metaphysical Lottery?"

"Assuming you know what a lottery is, let's examine the word metaphysical."

"For the audience's clarification, let's do."

"A metaphysical experience," the wizard explained, as he rolled his eyes at the teenagers who were losing interest, "is an experience that transcends the limits of ordinary experiences into a reality outside of what can be discerned by our senses."

"O . . . kay," Ruby drawled. "And what's my prize? A trip to Disneyland? A virtual reality ride on a space capsule to Mars? A ticket to the 3-D version of Harry Potter?"

2

"No, **no**, my dear," he said. He untied a red ribbon from a large roll of parchment, unfurled it theatrically, and held it up to the audience who were now throwing popcorn and flicking fingers dipped in their sugary drinks, completely oblivious to the announcer.

"You . . . what did you say your name is, my dear?"

She pointed to her name on the parchment.

"Oh, yes. You, Ruby Louise Holliday, are the lucky recipient of the most outrageous prize ever offered to any living person in the universe. I am proud to present the metaphysical experience of a lifetime! You may choose any person, living or dead, male or female, to trade places with," he paused . . . "for one fortnight!" He beamed and with a hammy sweep, handed the proclamation to Ruby Louise.

"Oh, I get it. This is a dream!"

"No, no, no! This is *not* a dream. This, my dear, is a metaphysical experience."

"I know a dream when I'm in it. This is a dream. That explains my swimsuit, and *you*. I'll wake up and won't even remember. I know how dreams work."

"And how will you explain this document with your name right here?" He pointed with a stubby finger at *Ruby Louise Holliday* written in loopy cursive with curlicues and flourishes.

"This is a fun dream so let me get this straight. You're saying I can be someone of my choice for two weeks? Will I look like the person I choose? What will happen to the me who works at Pet City six days a week? Will I just be gone?"

"Remember, this is a metaphysical experience. Since you can't be in two places at the same time . . . can you take two weeks off from your job?"

"I *knew* there'd be a 'but'. Okay, in the spirit of the joke, how long do I have to make my choice?"

"One day?" the wizard proposed.

"Oh sure," Ruby Louise said sarcastically.

The next morning the dream lingered in her mind. Musings of who she would choose to be, tickled as she showered. Julia Robert's willowy frame and infectious laugh? Probably eats celery sticks with lemon juice for every meal.

She coaxed some semblance of style into her brown hair and wondered how it would feel to be as beautiful as Gwen Stefani. She'd always considered herself a four.

"Why am I thinking about the stupid dream?" she asked as she applied powder to her freckled complexion. A quick stroke of eyeliner set off her large brown eyes. Besides, she concluded as she brushed her teeth, I wouldn't want to be a celebrity, except maybe Meryl Streep. She dressed for work while eating her breakfast. The pet store dress code was casual but no jeans.

*Chinos are about as attractive as clown pants . . . I need to stop thinking about that dream.*

Ruby Louise finished dressing, rinsed her bowl, and stacked it on the wire rack. She smoothed the sheet and duvet on her double bed. At twenty-four, she knew her job wasn't a career, but she hadn't gotten around to an associate degree as a veterinarian assistant.

On the bus, her mind couldn't leave 'what if' alone. The queen of England. Wouldn't that be a hoot? No. Margaret Mead? No.

At work, requests for the best gerbil food and to open the bird cage box and put the cage together kept Ruby too busy to daydream, but mid-morning in the break room, she found her friend Keesha sipping a diet Dr. Pepper.

"Keesha, if you could turn into anybody in the world for two weeks, who would you choose?"

"That's easy. I would be Alicia Keyes. She's smart, an excellent singer, and is so pretty, she doesn't wear make-up. Why? Do you have a magic wand?"

"No, it's just hypothetical. I can't decide who I would be."

"Well honey, answer the question before you meet your fairy godmother." Keesha finished her drink, rose from the white plastic chair, tossed the can in the recycle barrel, and left the break room, derriere swaying in her chinos.

Easy for her to say. Ruby nibbled her vending machine health bar, and despite her determination to forget the dream, names popped into her mind. Oprah. Ellen. Kim. She shook her head after each one.

The rest of the work day passed without the question nagging at her. On the ride home, the bus ground to a halt. The driver turned to face the passengers. "Bad accident ahead, folks. We'll be here a while. If we're close to your stop, you might want to walk the rest of the way."

Ruby Louise looked at the street ahead. Four blocks to her building. "I'll walk," she said.

"Just don't look," the driver warned as he opened the door.

The street was full of emergency vehicles, fire trucks, and half the police force, all flashing their lights. Sitting on the curb were a man in a suit and a child. The little boy was sobbing. His dad hugged him, tears streamed down his grief-stricken face. Ruby didn't look, but her mind's eye saw a wife and mother covered with a sheet.

"Crap, crap, crap," she said under her breath and marched to her building, barely able to keep her emotions under control. In her apartment, she splashed water on her face and poured a glass of wine. She took it to the bedroom, and sitting on the side of her bed, she untied her sneakers and reached underneath for her slippers.

Her fingers touched something that definitely wasn't a slipper. She dropped to her knees. With shaking hands, she pulled it out and unrolled the document.

10th Annual Metaphysical Lottery winner,

*Ruby Louise Holliday*

# Chapter 2

No alarm. *Must be Sunday.* Ruby Louise rolled over and snuggled into her pillow, hoping to continue the gallop down a beach on her jet-black horse.

The dream wouldn't come back. She opened one eye. Sunlight strained against the closed blinds, shooting two shafts of brilliance into the room where the slats didn't meet the casing. She gave in to the inevitability of morning and wondered about the many horses in her nighttime adventures.

As she swung her legs over the bed's edge, her cell phone trilled its birdcall ring. Eight o'clock on the dot. *Who would call so early on a Sunday morning?*

"Ruby Louise, where are you? You'd better be on your way. It's the busiest day of the week and the store's filling up." It was her supervisor, Mr. Boone.

"I don't work on Sunday." You idiot, she added under her breath.

"It's Saturday! Get your . . . get down here now!" Mr. Boone's voice bellowed through the tiny speaker.

No shower, no brushed teeth, she threw on yesterday's chinos and Pet City logo shirt, pulled on sneakers as she hopped down the hall and slammed out the door, barely remembering to grab her purse.

Running, she caught the bus and sank into a seat by a woman and her small child, eating a jelly doughnut. Tiny red, drippy, jelly-smeared hands threatened her chinos. Ruby scanned the bus for a different seat. Nothing. She cringed as far away from the child as possible. Mr. Boone would be apoplectic if she showed up looking like she'd been in a knife fight on top of being late.

To her relief, the woman and child got off at the next stop—the site where the terrible wreck had taken the life of a wife and a mother. Bits of metal and glass sparkled in the gutter. Her brain replayed the vision of the man and child sitting on the curb. Ruby hung her head. Death sucks. Why can't it only take out sociopaths?

After exiting at her stop, she marched through the glass door into Pet City ready to take her chastisement. No Mr. Boone in sight. She tossed her purse into a locker in the break room, cruised the aisles, and helped a woman hoist a fifty-pound bag of kibble into her cart. Two aisles over, she dipped a specifically chosen angelfish into a carton for a young girl.

"Oh, hello Mr. Boone. Sorry I was late. I thought it was—"

"You're on clean-up today," he said curtly and walked away.

Armed with the supplies apron, it wasn't long until she got the summons. "PICK-UP ON AISLE SEVEN." Ruby found an elderly lady holding the leash of the smallest Chihuahua she'd ever seen.

"I'm so sorry, dear. I don't know why Bruiser did that."

Bruiser had left a pile of poo a Mastiff would be proud of. Then, he'd peed on it. Ruby pulled on disposable rubber gloves, kneeled, and began the pick-up. A pair of oversized yellow clown shoes appeared inches from the mess. Her eyes traveled up the skinny, sock-clad ankles to the yellow and black checked pants.

"Ruby Louise. Come with me," the clown announced. Reverb ricocheted the sound off the walls of the large store. The little old lady and Bruiser didn't notice.

She jumped up, still holding the dripping poo. "You can't come here now. I'm working!" she whispered. "You'll get me fired."

"Yes, I can." He took her hand, now somehow empty. Ruby found she couldn't resist. They glided down the aisle as if they were on roller skates. She looked back and saw herself kneeling on the floor, still cleaning up dog poo.

They glided past the cat cages toward a desk and chair. In front of the desk was a ruffled, chintz-covered stool.

"Look, Mr. Whatever, we can't do this here. I'll lose my job."

"No, you won't. Sit. We'll get this sorted out and start you on your experience."

A couple walked by, oblivious to the impromptu office. They stopped at the parakeet enclosure.

"Pick out the one you want, Ellie. I'll go find a clerk." The man cast his eyes around, didn't see any help, and left the aisle.

"Are we invisible?" Ruby asked. "What do I call you?"

"We're not invisible. They just don't see us. You may call me Professor Mozart."

"Is that your real name?"

"No, but it's nice, isn't it?"

She rolled her eyes. "You're a silly man. I can't take you seriously in that clown get-up." In one blink, Professor Mozart changed his clown persona into the wizard, with grey herringbone pants and a gold brocade vest over a white shirt. Above his blue eyes sat a shiny black top hat.

Ruby didn't notice the change. Her eyes were on the couple at the parakeet enclosure. Catching net in hand, her other self, pointed to a green bird. Ellie shook her head. The birds were squawking and flying blindly into each other and Ruby Louise in a blue and green chaos.

"That one, that one," Ellie called, pointing to a blue one on the floor. Ruby watched herself neatly net the bird, clasp it, and squeeze out of the back of the enclosure. Bird droppings decorated her logo shirt and chinos, a juicy one trickled on her cheek, and a few tiny precious feathers lodged in her hair.

"Yikes! I need to find a better job. Oh, you look better, Professor." She refused to call him Mozart.

"I'm a busy man, my dear. Please seat yourself so we may proceed. Have you chosen who you would like to be for the next two weeks?"

"Yes, but I have some questions. Where will I live? Will I stay in this city? If I don't like being who I chose, will I be able to abort?"

"Yes, yes, I'll answer your questions but first you must tell me who you chose to be. Don't be fearful. This will be a wonderful experience."

Ruby had her doubts but she'd made up her mind.

"One question, Professor. Is anyone off-limits?"

"No, no. This is a metaphysical experience. The sky's the limit."

"Okay. I want to be the Angel of Death."

# Chapter 3

"The Grim Reaper?" Professor Wizard put a finger to each ear and wiggled them while squinting his eyes shut.

"Not Grim Reaper," Ruby Louise corrected. "The Angel of Death."

"My dear, they're one and the same."

"You said the sky was the limit. I've made my choice. Do I get my experience, or not?"

The professor looked at her determined face, sighed, and opened a desk drawer on his right.

"Howard Hughes," he mumbled. "Cindi Lauper, Yogi Berra, Michelle Obama, Mae West ... someone should alphabetize these. Oh, here it is. Death. You're sure you don't want to be any of those?" he asked.

"The Angel of Death."

Professor Wizard pulled a fat folder from the drawer, opened it, and one by one, examined each document at length.

Ruby put her elbows on the desk, rested her chin on clasped hands, and closed her eyes. She couldn't be called a beauty. Wide temples led to a pointy chin, white skin that freckled, and hair that barely missed being red, were legacies from her Irish father. Eyes that couldn't decide to be green or brown were from the grandmother she'd never met.

*What's taking so long? I have so many questions and he's deliberately dithering. Doddering old fart. Come on. Let's get this show on the road.*

He looked up, scrutinizing her. "Ruby Louise, may I ask why you chose Death?"

She searched his eyes. "Why? It's kind of personal."

"Death is a powerful act. Catastrophic in the wrong hands. You don't look like a serial killer, but I can't turn just anybody loose with the power of Death. You've heard of the plague in the Middle Ages? Caused by a vindictive Grim Reaper."

"I get it," she said. "But I could tell you a frothy lie about wanting to save . . . say the butterflies from hitting windshields. You'd say, Okay. And then I could wipe out every bully on every school ground."

"My dear, I may look like a doddering old fart, but I have," he paused, "The Second Sight. The second sight. The second sight." The echo bounced off the walls and finally ended in a murmur.

Ruby looked at him, wide-eyed. "How'd you do that?"

"Did you like it?" The wizard beamed. "It was good, wasn't it?"

She sighed. "Sorry about the old fart thing. I suppose you can read my mind."

"More than that. Butterflies have their own Angel. All animals do."

He picked up the file, suddenly all business, refiled it and opened the drawer in front of him. "This is the key to your apartment." He laid it on the desk. "You'll have your own driver, Abdul. He'll be in a regular cab. Can't attract attention, ya know."

"So I'm in? I'm the Angel of Death?"

"Actually, that position is filled and he's very busy with that thing in the Middle East, so now isn't a good time for him to take two weeks off. What *is* available is a position as an Angel. You'll love it. No messy blood or guts, you know."

"Just an Angel? Wait! What does an Angel do? Do I flit around with wings growing out of my back? I'm afraid of heights. No! This won't work!"

The wizard laid his stubby hand on hers. "Angels are the most important beings in the entire metaphysical realm. No wings, no flitting, and no heights. Just an ordinary-looking person with extraordinary powers. You'll be able to change people's lives for far, far better outcomes. What do you say, Ruby Louise?"

She thought of the scene she'd witnessed of herself in the parakeet enclosure. Angel or Mr. Boone's flunky?

"Okay, I'll try it for two weeks."

"Oh, good. Here comes your assistant."

Ruby frowned. "I don't really want an assistant."

She swiveled and saw a small brown dog trotting over. He jumped nimbly onto her lap, gave her cheek a lick, and settled down, chin resting on her knee.

"Look, Wizard. I love dogs as much as the next guy, but this isn't a great time to become a pet owner. I'll be too busy to walk him, bathe him, buy dog food . . . an Angel picking up dog poo off the sidewalk?"

The dog picked up his head and gave her a knowing look. His brown eyes were rimmed with black like the best smoky-eye make-up women paid good money to achieve.

"He understood me, didn't he? Does he have second sight too?"

"All dogs have second sight. Buster has *third* sight. He'll help you in ways you'll understand when you embark on your adventure."

Ruby shrugged. "I suppose . . . no offense, Buster. I'm sure you're a nice dog."

Buster laid his chin on her knee and closed his eyes.

"Any more surprises before I go?"

"Your appearance. You can't be Ruby Louise, pet store worker and Ruby Louise, Angel, can you? When you enter your new apartment, look in the full-length mirror. You'll get three choices. If you don't like the first image, snap your fingers. If you want to see your third choice, snap again. There's clothing in the closet."

He took an iPhone out of the drawer. "This is your signaling device for when you're needed. When you're summoned, you must respond. Your jurisdiction is inside the city limits. See this icon on the home page? That's fifty-seven commandments you need to learn by heart."

"Fifty-seven commandments!" Her voice rose to a shrill pitch.

Buster looked at the wizard and gave a low growl.

"Perfect!" the wizard crowed. "The demonstration of his powers. He signaled that I told a lie. There are only five commandments. Good job, Buster."

Buster jumped to the floor and danced around.

"He's saying it's time to go. Here's his leash and his poo baggies. Good luck, Ruby Louise. My number is in your phone under M for Mozart."

In a swirl of air, the desk, chairs and the wizard were gone.

"Come on, Buster. Let's go be Angels."

# Chapter 4

A cab waited in a parking place in front of Pet City. It was bright yellow and a little scruffy with scratches and a minor dent on the back fender. The driver was also a little scruffy. He wore a baseball cap that a more fastidious man would have thrown away. He unfolded his tall, skinny frame, climbed out, and opened the rear door.

"Are you Abdul?"

"Yes, Miss." He smiled a snaggle-toothed grin.

"Do you know where to take me?" she asked as he jack-knifed his body behind the wheel.

"Yes, Miss." He executed a U-turn and pulled into traffic.

Ruby Louise realized she'd left her purse in a locker at Pet City. After a few seconds of panic, she sank back in her seat. Angels don't need purses . . . she hoped.

The interior of the cab was quite luxurious. Spotless dove-grey velour upholstery, pointy glass vases hung on both sides, filled with fresh Daisies, Lilies of the Valley, and blue Shooting Stars.

"Wow, Buster. This is nice."

Buster, who had chosen to catch a nap, raised his head, yawned, and returned to his doggy dream, the bunny that plagued his sleep.

"Where are we going, Abdul?"

"City center, Miss. See that tall building? You'll be on the top floor."

Abdul pulled into the underground parking and parked close to the elevator in a restricted space.

"Will they allow Buster? It looks snooty."

"Yes, Miss. Your private elevator has an "A" above it. It stops in your apartment. I'm on call 24/7. Push zero on your phone. By the time you get to the parking garage, I'll have the car door open for you."

"Huh. I hope they're paying you well, Abdul."

"Yes, Miss. Don't worry about me." He pointed to the "A" elevator.

"Abdul, the next time you see me, I'll look completely different."

He gave a knowing nod.

"Come on, Buster." He jumped to the concrete and trotted to the elevator. The door opened as Ruby Louise walked up to it. She looked at Abdul. "Did you do that?"

"Face recognition. Your new look will be recorded. It's all been factored."

"What do *you* say, Buster?" He trotted into the elevator and wagged his tail. No growl. Abdul told the truth.

The ascent to the thirty-sixth floor was smooth. The door opened and Ruby looked into her temporary home. *It's huge.* A glass wall illuminated the room. She stepped onto the pale grey carpet and sank into the plush. A deep blue sofa wrapped around the room, the longest sofa she'd ever seen.

She sat on the floor and took off her sneakers. "Let's explore, Buster."

They walked to the kitchen. Dark stainless-steel appliances. She opened the refrigerator. A papaya, two English cucumbers, gruyere cheese, a jar of Kalamata olives, Greek yogurt, and three bottles of Kim Crawford white wine. Her stomach growled.

They walked along the glass wall to the bedroom. The bed was as large as the entire bedroom in her apartment. Warm apricot walls set off the deep red bedspread. A large abstract painting arrested Ruby Louise's scan. Two bold swatches of midnight blue gradually softened into ultramarine, intercepted by a dazzling white shape that faded into the sky-colored background. *Wow.*

She turned and saw the gold-framed mirror. *Why am I nervous about this? What if the choices are grotesque and ugly? Courage, Ruby. Angels can't be squeamish.*

"Here goes nothing, Buster." He jumped onto the bed and sank to his belly, muzzle resting on his paws. His eyes stayed on her.

She took a deep breath and stepped in front of the mirror.

"Huh." The woman in the image seemed familiar. "Oh! I know." She reminded her of Angelina Jolie who played those seductive but tough roles. Her iconic full lips gave her away. Ruby turned and the image turned. Angelina did the same. Ruby raised her arms in a karate stance, hands flat and menacing.

"This is wild, Buster!" She snapped her fingers and Angelina disappeared. In her place stood a gorgeous, curvaceous woman, a blond Sofia Vergara.

"Oh my." The mouth moved in sync.

Ruby slowly pulled off her Pet City polo. She stepped out of her chinos.

"Close your eyes, Buster."

She unhooked the bra which wasn't up to its new job. Two perfect melons tumbled out, taking Ruby's breath away. Slowly, she pulled open the elastic of her white cotton panties.

17

"Do you want to be an Angel?" she asked her newly blond coochie.

That was fun. Who's next? She snapped her fingers. She looked older, forty-ish. Kind of motherly. Ruby picked up her bra and put it back on. Sandy-blond hair in a conservative style. Not feminine or masculine. A little like Martha Stewart.

"I'll fix you a beebleberry, sour cream compote, and you'll be eternally happy," Ruby Louise and the Martha look-alike said.

Buster jumped off the bed and stood beside her, looking in the mirror. He still looked like Buster. She laughed. "Buster, I'm too hungry to make a decision. After lunch, you can help me decide between toughie, sexy, or motherly."

Ruby Louise and Martha left the mirror.

In the kitchen, she made herself an eggplant, Spanish manchego cheese sandwich on toasted ciabatta bread.

"Wait! I'm not going to eat this. It's changed into Martha Stewart food. I haven't made my choice."

She slammed the plate down and ran to the bedroom. In front of the mirror, stood Martha in Ruby's panties and bra.

"No-o-o-o!" she yelled. "I didn't choose you!"

# Chapter 5

Buster and Ruby stood in front of the mirror. "It isn't that I *don't* choose you, Martha. It's just that I haven't chosen yet." She snapped her fingers. Nothing happened.

"Holy crap," she said quietly.

"This is *my* metaphysical experience. I have a document. I CHOOSE SOFIA!"

She snapped her fingers and peeked.

The blond look-alike of Sofia Vergara looked out of the mirror. Ruby and the blonde woman snapped their fingers together. Nothing. They snapped again. No change. Ruby walked away from the image. She looked down at her bra. The stitches were popping.

"Why did I choose Sofia, Buster?" she giggled. "It's so not me."

After the best night's sleep she'd ever had, Ruby woke, wondered where she was, and rolled onto her back. She caught sight of movement across the room and when she rose onto her elbows, she saw a blonde woman leaning on *her* elbows looking at her! They froze. Then she saw Buster, watching another Buster. It all came back to her.

"Buster, I scared myself," she said. "I'm not sure I *like* looking so different. It's creepy."

Her 'Call to Arms' phone blared a jazzed version of "Mary Had a Little Lamb." Ruby realized it was her first summons.

"Crap, Buster. I'm not dressed!" She rushed to the walk-in closet and stepped in. With a whoosh, she was instantly dressed completed with shoes and lacy underwear. "I didn't even get to see my choices. Oh, well. Let's go, Buster. We have work to do."

She glanced at the mirror as they rushed by. Short yellow skirt, miles of shapely leg, strappy espadrilles, and an ivory-colored blouse with peek-a-boo shoulders and yellow buttons that stopped short of a display of cleavage. She stopped.

"I need to change clothes, Buster. I don't look like an Angel."

Buster gave a sharp bark, rushed into the living room, and danced in front of the elevator.

"Right. No time." She followed. "Who made you the boss, Buster?"

The doors slid open, and she stepped in. *My first assignment. I might be good at this job.*

When the elevator doors slid open again, Abdul stood at the cab, holding the back door open. Buster jumped in after Ruby and put his chin on her lap. A black, wispy Fu-Man-Chu hung off his furry, little brown muzzle.

"Morning, Miss." Abdul wore oversized aviators and a colorful Hawaiian shirt.

"Good morning, Abdul. Where are we going?"

He glided into traffic.

"West side of town, Miss. A bachelor needs help. We're here," Abdul said. Just seconds had passed.

He pulled into a driveway, winding through boulders, and native oak. The house, built of oiled logs, stone, and glass, looked like it had grown out of the hill. Boulders, as big as Volkswagen beetles snuggled next to the home.

Abdul opened Ruby's door. She climbed out.

"Come on, Buster. Time to roll."

He opened his mouth in a big, yawn, stretched, and finally stood.

"You sure you need me?"

"Oh! . . . Was that you, Buster? You . . . can talk?"

"Of course I can talk! All dogs talk."

"Why . . . didn't I hear you before?"

"I didn't say anything. Are you sure you need me? I'm tired."

"I certainly *do* need you! We're a team."

Buster picked his way to the edge of the seat and flopped down.

"Whistle if you really need me. I'll wait here."

"Oh, for crying out loud." Ruby picked Buster up and set him on the ground. She walked up the chip-wood path to the steps.

"Don't ever do that again," Buster growled. "I *hate* to be picked up. I was going to jump. You didn't give me a chance." He grumbled all the way up the steps to the door.

Ruby rapped the horseshoe door knocker. There was no response. She knocked again. She tried the doorknob. Locked.

"I wish we could go through walls, Buster. That would be helpful."

"I think we can. Try it," he growled.

"Really?"

"Yeah. Just step into it like it isn't there."

Ruby hesitated and two steps later crashed into the door with her nose.

"Ow, ow! That hurt." She touched her nose. Her finger came away bloody.

"I'm bleeding, Buster." She turned to let him see her scraped nose.

"Well, it was worth a try. Want me to lick that for you?"

Ruby dabbed her nose with the shirttail of her blouse.

"You set me up. That was mean."

Buster trotted away. "Let's look for a doggy door. I smell a dog."

Ruby followed him around the house.

"Ornery mutt," she grumbled. "My nose could have been broken."

"Here it is. Even you could get through this, Ruby. A big dog lives here."

"Well, what are you waiting for, Buster? Go in."

"No way. I'm just a little guy. You go first."

Ruby sat down on the step and pulled out the flap. She peeked in to see if a snarling attack animal waited. A pointy nose poked out and a long red tongue slurped across her face, getting dog spit in her mouth. A second nose joined the fun but Ruby dropped the flap.

"Poodles," she sputtered, spitting and wiping her mouth on her shirtsleeve.

"Well, poodles can be vicious," Buster whined.

Ruby was already inserting herself into the dog door, feet first. Two tall, black, standards danced around her, happy to see a benefactor.

"You can come in, Buster. These guys are glad to see us."

He poked his head in. "They're probably going to trample me."

The dog entrance opened into a service room. Two bowls and a large, crock water dish were empty. Ruby found a bin of kibbles, scooped until their bowls were full, and filled their water dish.

"Come on, Buster. The bachelor's waiting for us."

They entered the kitchen. Granite counters and windowed cupboards showing cobalt-blue stoneware. The glasses and stemware matched, unlike Ruby's thrift-shop acquisitions. Copper-clad cookware hung on a wrought-iron pot hook. No food smells lingered.

Must have a cleaning crew, she mused, but why weren't the dogs fed?

Ruby hurried through the great room, admiring the soaring open-beam ceiling, the wall of glass, and the massive, native-rock fireplace. The floor was irregular-width pecan-wood planks. Ruby skirted the oversized, stuffed furniture. Buster followed his nose and entered a wide hall that led to a spacious bedroom. He jumped onto the foot of the bed.

"Who the hell are you?" the man croaked as Ruby entered the room.

"I'm an Angel. I'm here to help you."

"Oh yeah?" His gravelly voice was little more than a whisper. "Prove it."

She could tell that, at one time, the man had been handsome. Dark hair curled around a face that was skin stretched on bone. She had never seen such an emaciated person.

"You need a doctor. You're sick."

"Sick of living. I just want it all to end," he whispered.

Dark brown eyes, large in their cavernous sockets stared at her. The man's legs barely showed under the thin cotton blanket.

The poodles, finished with their dinners, ran into the room. They rose on their hind legs to the side of the bed. The man stretched a feeble arm to them. They joyously licked his hand.

"What are their names?" Ruby asked.

"Duchess and Duke. When they're old enough . . ." His voice trailed off.

"You'll be dead. Is that your plan?"

The man slowly turned his head and stared.

"What's your name?" she said. "Mine's Ruby Louise."

"You said you're an Angel. What're you waiting for? Take me out."

"Are your dogs part of your plan? Starve them to death too?"

A tear trickled down his cheek and landed on the blanket. Ruby picked up his skin-and-bones hand and held it in her own.

"Buster, would you go look at his mail and find out his name for me?"

Ruby shook her head. *I'm an Angel who's ignorant of what the job calls for. I'm in way over my head.*

Buster came in with an envelope in his mouth. He jumped on the bed and spat it out. Ruby wiped it on her skirt and turned it over.

"Mike Harrington! You're the anchorman on the news channel! I've seen you hundreds of times. You were a shoo-in for the Mayor of Denver until you mysteriously dropped out of the race. You're enormously popular, Mike Harrington. Everybody admires you. Including me."

Mike's eyes slowly opened. "Are you going to do it, or not?"

"I'm *not* the Angel of Death."

She looked down at the black poodles.

"Mike, you have two loving dogs. Are you okay with them being collateral damage to your escape plan?"

Long silence.

"I hired a kid to come in and feed them," he whispered.

"*You're* their life support. Eventually, someone would come here and find you and these sweet dogs starved to death. Or worse. Dogs driven to starvation sometimes eat any—"

"Stop!" he said louder. "I get it. *You* take them. Is that what you want?"

24

"Here's my plan," Ruby said. "I'll send out a nutritionist. You can afford it. She'll get you back on your feet enough so you can find homes for them. Good homes, not just dumped off at the county pound. Personally interview the potentials. Go see their yards. Make sure they aren't going to chain them up and leave them without human company. Someone to take care of them like you would if you . . ."

"Hadn't taken the chicken-shit way out? You don't know me," he spat.

"No, I don't. Does anyone know you're this desperate? Maybe, Mike, it's time to let someone really know you."

"So, Miss *Angel*," he snarled. "you also dabble in amateur psychoanalysis?" His voice, heavy with sarcasm, struck her funny bone. She couldn't keep a laugh in.

Mike painfully turned his head and glared. "What's so funny?"

"Nothing. This is a tragedy." Ruby burst out in another giggle. "I'm sorry. It's just that you do sarcasm so well."

"Want to hear some more?"

She smiled. "That was good, Mike, but I don't want to wear you out. Do you want a glass of water, a milkshake, a carrot? I'm so scared for you, I'm being silly."

She brought him a glass of water and a straw. He took a long drink and she put the glass on the bedside table.

"You *are* going to leave, aren't you?"

"I am. Your dogs are fine. I'll be back tomorrow. Do you have a key I can take? I came in through the dog flap."

"I thought you walked through the wall, ghost-like."

"I tried. See this raw place on my nose?"

A shadow of a smile played across Mike's face. "Very professional. What about this scruffy little mutt on my bed?"

"Tell him, Buster."

25

Buster turned and gazed out the window.

"We're having issues. He's tired and grumpy today."

"Key's on a hook beside the back door. Now get out of here."

"Bye, Mike. See you tomorrow. Remember the new plan."

Ruby circled her arm over Mike's wasted body.

"What was that for?" he grunted.

"I felt like sprinkling you with a little Angel juju."

When she and Buster reached the cab, she climbed into the front seat.

"I need to talk to you, Abdul, face to face."

# Chapter 6

Abdul didn't start the engine. He didn't prompt her. She skooched down, leaned her head on the seat, and stared out the windshield, focused on nothing. The silence stretched on.

"I'm scared, Abdul," she finally said.

"Tell me."

She looked at him. "Can anyone stop a desperate person from committing suicide?"

She put her hands over her face. "I don't want him to die. This is too big for me. I need help."

"Is he in immediate danger?"

"*I don't know!* I appealed for him to stay alive for the love of his dogs. At least long enough to find good homes for them. He could make a phone call and then slit his wrists. He could be doing it right now. I have no power to stop him." She choked down a sob. "I'm a lousy Angel."

"Ruby, you did all you could for now. People have free will. It's how we're wired."

She gazed out the window in deep thought.

"Okay, I need a non-angel to come here tomorrow and become his best friend. Preferably a pretty, single woman, between twenty-five and thirty-five, who's empathetic and a good listener, can live in, and prepare tasty food to get him back on his feet. She should appreciate sarcasm. And love dogs."

"That's a tall order for tomorrow. Any candidates in mind?"

"None. Oh, Abdul. What am I going to do? I can't stand the thought that this accomplished, agonized man might erase himself while I do nothing."

"Do you realize that the woman you described is you? Other than being a non-angel."

Ruby stared into Abdul's dark eyes.

He started the engine and followed the circle drive back onto the street.

"It's been a long day. I'll take you and Buster back to your apartment. Think about it overnight. It may mean losing the rest of your Angel tenure. It's up to you."

She went to bed early but tossed and turned. Nightmares plagued her sleep. Each bad dream woke her. She rolled onto her side but her mind continued to play disturbing scenarios.

How did they get along without me before? Was there an Angel that cared as much as I care? She thought about waking Buster to ask him but he might still be miffed about being picked up.

She got out of bed and padded into the living room. Blue moonlight streamed through the glass wall, strong and calming. She sat on the carpet, leaned against the sofa, and stretched out her legs. Her mind wouldn't stop.

Why am I in such a twist over this? It's past midnight. This is my first day. Thirteen days left. Do I have any special Angel powers? Why didn't I ask the wizard? I've gotten a humdinger of a new look, a willful mutt, and a luxury apartment . . . but all this can't help me save Mike from himself.

I should quit. Slink back to Pet City and get my job back. Maybe they haven't missed me yet. I could show up in my logo shirt and chinos and . . . oh, right. I don't look like Pet City Ruby Louise anymore.

What do other people do when they can't make a decision? Ask a psychic? I don't have a Ouija board. Maybe meditate.

Ruby put a couch pillow behind her neck, closed her eyes, relaxed, and emptied her mind. She went to sleep.

When she opened her eyes, sunlight streamed in. Buster sat looking at her. She stretched, looked around, and remembered why she was on the living room floor.

"It worked, Buster."

"What?"

"Meditation. I couldn't decide whether to become a non-angel and try to save Mike H. from himself, or finish my thirteen days as the Angel, help lots of people, and not worry about saving just one suicidal guy."

"So?"

"Let's eat breakfast first. I'm starving. I know you are, too."

Ruby sang bits and pieces of "Yellow Submarine" as she fried bacon and beat four eggs to a froth. With bread in the toaster, she mixed kibble, scrambled eggs, and bacon bits into Buster's dish. He was done with his feast by the time Ruby sat at the table to eat her breakfast.

"Okay, I'm done," he said after a last lick of his bowl. "Tell me."

"Don't try to talk me out of this decision, Buster. I know people commit suicide all the time, so other Angels don't stop them. I can't save everybody, but maybe I can save Mr. Harrington. It's a gamble, but if I don't try, he'll succeed. I'd be responsible. I've got to try."

"You'll be there every day. I'm not cut out for that. I resign. You're on your own, Kiddo."

"Buster, I need you. Please stay with me."

"Nope."

"That's all you have to say? No apology?"

29

"Yep."

"I'll never pick you up again. Please reconsider. I need you, Buster!"

"Oh . . . okay."

Ruby's phone rang her personal ring, saving her from responding.

"It's me," Abdul said. "May I come up?"

"Let yourself in, Abdul. I'll be ready in ten minutes."

Ruby took one more bite of scrambled eggs and hurried to her room. As she showered, her head was a maelstrom of unknowns. She felt queasy as she toweled dry.

She chose natural linen pants and a raspberry-hued top. She stepped into a pair of strappy sandals.

"Just a few more minutes, Abdul." she called.

"Buster told me," Abdul said when she walked into the living room. "I wasn't surprised."

Ruby looked around the room, planning to throw the little brown dog a kiss.

"Where is he?"

"He won't be back, Ruby. An Angel's job is to touch down, help people in need, and then go on. You'll no longer be fulfilling the Angel position so you won't need an assistant. Painless, wasn't it?"

She shook her head, frowned, and looked troubled.

"Do you want to change your mind? There's still time . . . it's up to you." Abdul gave her a sympathetic look, took off his baseball cap, and twisted it.

"No. We need to get to his house," Ruby said. "Now!"

They hurried to the cab. It felt wrong that Buster wasn't with them.

When they pulled into Mike's driveway, Abdul turned off the engine and looked at her.

"Abdul, I'm homeless and penniless since I walked out on my Pet City job and my apartment. What if Mike kicks me out?"

"No, Ruby. Your clothes from the suite will be delivered later today. There is a consequence to your abdication. If you'd stayed for the full two weeks, we would have paid you ten thousand dollars for your service. Now, we don't have an Angel for the next thirteen days. You forfeited your per-diem, but you have a job *here*. He needs you. Charge Mike double the minimum personal caregiver wage for however many days you're here. He can afford it. You won't get rich, but you won't be destitute."

Ruby looked out the window and considered Abdul's solution. She wondered if she could convince Mike to pay her for butting into his death.

"Okay. I'll miss you and Buster, though."

"If you're up for doing special assignments in the future, we'll see each other again."

"I'll think about it. Can I give you a hug now that I'm not an Angel?"

Impulsively, Ruby reached for Abdul. Her hands and arms slid through him without feeling anything. She sat back abruptly and looked at him in disbelief. "You're . . ."

"Just as real as you, but in a different dimension," he said. "Did you forget you've been living a metaphysical existence?"

"Is this really happening, Abdul? Do you actually exist?"

"Absolutely. Now, go save Mike Harrington. I'm confident that you'll succeed, Ruby."

Abdul opened her door and Ruby climbed out for the last time. She looked up at the stone and log house and took a deep breath. She turned to throw Abdul an air-kiss but he and the cab were gone. She looked down the curved driveway. No dust lingered and no crunch of gravel could be heard.

# Chapter 7

Ruby marched up the path, circled to the side door, and let herself in with the key. Duke and Duchess danced around her. "Come on, troops. Let's go see Mike."

She found him in the living room. He looked like a scarecrow that had lost its straw. He was dressed in jeans and a tee-shirt.

"What are *you* here for?" he asked.

"To be your friend. I'll also cook, grocery shop, take friendly abuse, and talk a lot. I'm a good listener. My name's Ruby Louise, but you can call me Ruby. Yesterday, you met me as an Angel."

"Go away," he said, dully.

"Okay. Have you had breakfast?"

"Are you hearing impaired? I said, GO AWAY!"

"Okay." She skipped into the kitchen. "Bullying doesn't bother me," she called cheerfully.

The food in the refrigerator had gone limp, sour, or moldy, weeks ago. The freezer side was more promising. Two large tubs of vanilla ice cream, a bag of mixed fruit, six pizzas, and an unopened cheesecake. She took it out and read the directions. Thaw and eat.

Mike's kitchen was appliance-rich. She put the cheesecake in the microwave. When it was soft enough to cut, she put a quarter of it into the blender, dumped in some of the frozen fruit, and topped it off with a generous amount of ice cream. She switched it on high and walked away.

Ruby belted out "Jolene" as she threw all the neglected food from the refrigerator into the bin.

She turned off the blender. The smoothie was too thick and too cold.

In the pantry, she found a case of bottled coffee drinks.

He likes coffee, he gets coffee. She poured one bottle into the blender. The mixture slowly changed to pale tan. She tried it. "Even Mikey'll like it," she told Duke and Duchess, who watched with interest.

"Maybe," Ruby heard as she put straws into the drinks. She turned and looked around the room. Only the dogs were there.

Duke sat down, picked up his back foot, and scratched his neck. Duchess sniffed something on the floor. Ruby frowned. "That was weird," she muttered.

"Breakfast, coming up, Darlin'." Ruby walked into the living room with two large glasses, each with a fat straw.

"One for you and one for me." She put his down on the side table and sat on the extended couch.

"Mike, do you have a ghost in the house with a French accent?"

"I hate smoothies," Mike snarled.

"This is a milkshake. Take a sip."

"No."

"If you take a sip, I'll do you a favor."

"Leave?"

She laughed. "You're a master of snarky, Mike. Take a sip and you'll find out."

Ruby took a sip. "M-m m! I love coffee. I bet you miss your morning coffee."

34

She sneaked a peak. Despite his pissed-off expression, she saw him eye the drink. The idea of coffee seemed to drive a chink in his resistance.

Ruby handed the glass to him. "One sip," she said. "Okay, here's my favor."

"This morning when I woke, I was an Angel. Honest, Mike. True story. Now, I'm Ruby, an ordinary woman. Here's how it happened." She glanced toward Mike. He still held the milkshake.

Drink it, drink it, drink it, she chanted in her mind. To her amazement, he took the straw in his mouth and drew on it. He started to put it down and she chanted, drink more. He drank more. She could hardly believe it was her mind that caused him to drink, but still . . .

"Two days ago," Ruby picked up her story, "I worked for a pet store chain. It was my day off and I went to a movie. I bought a tub of popcorn and a large—"

"Be specific," Mike said. "What movie?"

"*Pet Cemetery.* As I was saying, I had a large *strawberry* slush and a tub of *buttered* popcorn. I found the perfect seat and as I sat down, I heard my name called on the loudspeaker."

She stole a quick look. The milkshake was down a half inch. Again, he started to set it down. Ruby chanted once more. Mike sipped again.

"That's when it got wonky," she went on.

"What's wonky? Define wonky."

"Skewed. Enigmatic, inexplicable. A clown on the movie theater stage announced that I, Ruby Louise Holliday, had won the tenth annual Metaphysical Lottery. He said to come down and collect my prize. It could have been a joke except when I looked down, I was shocked to see I had on an old, faded, blue swimsuit I'd thrown out two years earlier because the elastic in

35

the legs had gone south. That's when I knew reality had slipped a cog. *That's* wonky and it's just the beginning."

Mike put his glass down. It was half empty. Good enough for a guy who'd been on an extended fast.

"You look tired, Mike. Why don't you catch a nap? By the way, I'll order a few groceries so I need your credit card." She waited for the blast.

"My credit card! Are you crazy? I don't *know* you. What's to keep you from ordering diamond earrings or a new Ferrari? Do I look like a total idiot?"

"Wow! I could put a Ferrari on your credit card?"

Mike dropped his head into his hands. "Order what you need and bring me the receipt," he mumbled. "The card's in the top drawer of my desk. I'm going to rest."

The dogs were lying at his feet. Mike rose and walked unsteadily to his bedroom. Duchess brought a ball and dropped it in his path.

"Not now, Duchess. Maybe after more of those terrible milkshakes."

Ruby stood in the doorway of Mike's office with a grin. Wow. I think I made him eat a little. Take it slow, she cautioned herself. Let him snarl. Probably what he needs.

The office walls were a soft grey. The floor had the same pecan wood as the other rooms. A square rug depicted a trompe l'oeil scene of a mermaid poised in a deep blue pool, her tail fading away into the depth. Ruby skirted it and walked to the oak desk. No way will I ever step on that rug, she vowed.

Nice computer, cluttered desk. Two large paintings on the walls. A monochromatic oil of two sea lions swimming through a kelp forest. The other, an abstract so beautiful it gave her goosebumps. The suggestion of a wet, sandy beach, a hint of an ocean beyond, and the feeling of a rain-heavy sky, and small, fiery-orange slashes of color. The evocative painting kindled new appreciation of Mike.

Finally, she opened the desk drawer, and among the rubber bands and paper clips, she found the credit card.

Ruby tip-toed to Mike's bedroom and peeked around the door in case he was sleeping. He lay staring at the ceiling.

"Mike," she said softly, "where do you get your groceries, and do they deliver?"

"Ralphs. And the answer to your next invasion of my privacy is abracadabra. Anything else? My shoe size? Preference of boxers or jockeys?"

She laughed. You rascal, she thought. You're enjoying the curmudgeon act. I'll play along, and give it right back.

"Yes, now that you ask. Fixodent or Poligrip?"

Mike glared at her. Ruby's brows shot up. She maintained a deadpan expression.

"Get out of here before I sic Duke on you."

"Oh please, Mr. Harrington," she said in a falsetto voice. "Don't set your vicious dog on me."

Smiling, she stepped into the hall and heard, "I can be vicious," from behind her. She turned around. "Did you say something, Mike?"

"I *said* get out of here."

"I thought I heard something. I'll close your door. Come on, Duke."

He'd given her his computer password. It was a huge concession.

There was a knock on the door. "I'll get it," she called.

A khaki-clad stranger stood beside a stack of large cartons. "Where you want these?" the man grunted.

"Who are they for?"

He looked at his manifest. "Says Ruby. That you?"

"Yes. Just set them inside." Ruby signed the paperwork and closed the door.

She walked past Mike's closed door and looked for another bedroom. It was down the hall on the opposite side and had its own bathroom. She hadn't asked if she could stay. He'd probably say no, so she just moved in.

Hanging her clothes in the closet, putting her shoes along the wall and undies on the shelves, she felt a sharp tug of regret for her lost Angel job, plus the ten thousand dollars she'd forfeited when she dropped out of her post early.

The smallest carton contained her cosmetics, toiletries, her collection of silver jewelry, and the sky-blue phone that would have summoned her to the Angel scenarios.

She thought about Abdul and Buster. I knew them too briefly, and now they're gone. Lost to me forever.

Mr. Suicidal Curmudgeon is my sole focus. Why do I always choose these lonely missions? Confused and sad, she felt pulled apart. She crawled onto the bed and closed her eyes. Duke and Duchess jumped onto the bed and found their spots. When she drifted into half-sleep, she heard, "She'll do it."

"Shut up, Buster," she mumbled and slid into oblivion.

# Chapter 8

"Smell this shoe. It's yummy." Ruby woke from her nap to the sounds of snuffling in the closet. And talking?

"Hey, you nosy dogs, come here." She swung her legs over the side of the bed. The dogs sat on the rug next to her feet.

"Don't be shy. I'm not scolding you."

She didn't know if they could communicate with her like Buster had. "What do they smell like, Duke?"

"Cow, other places, and, you." He watched to see if she understood.

"Wow. I'm glad my nose doesn't work as well as yours." Ruby smiled and scratched both of their necks under their floppy ears.

"Okay, troops. Let's open Mike's computer. We need to get some nourishing food in this house." They danced around her as she walked barefoot to the office.

After finding the grocery shop Mike named, Ruby picked up her Angel phone and ordered organic fruit, some root vegetables, spinach, Greek yogurt, and, thinking of soup for dinner, added butternut squash, onions, garlic, and stock.

She wondered who kept his house dusted and cleaned. She poked a finger into the dirt of several large house plants that looked neglected. On her way to remedy their thirst, there was a loud knock at the door. A tall, skinny boy stood on the welcome mat with three large, brown paper bags.

"Nice house," he said, looking around as he came in. He had freckles and a mass of red, curly hair. He set the bags on the counter.

"I'm Ruby. What's your name?"

"You can call me Pete." She checked that all the items in the bag matched the receipt and handed him the credit card.

"Can I put a tip on the card, Pete?"

"No, Ma'am. It's against the store's rules to accept tips."

"Wait here." She hurried back to Mike's room and knocked softly on the closed door.

"What now?" he growled.

"Do you have a fiver so I can tip the delivery boy?" She held her breath.

"I suppose."

Ruby stepped into his room. The oversized bedroom furniture reminded her of a style she'd seen in a Colorado ski lodge brochure. She'd hardly noticed the décor the day before. The bedposts were thick tree limbs. The massive dresser he pointed to was the same natural wood with wrought-iron pulls. She picked up a tooled leather wallet and handed it to him. He fished out a bill.

Mike was still dressed in his jeans and tee. He'd slipped out of his leather moccasins and was lying on a maroon matelassé bedspread.

"When you get finished with him, come in here."

"Yes, SIR." She saluted and clicked her heels together.

"Smart ass."

She handed Pete the tip. "I'll be calling for more groceries soon. Probably tomorrow."

"Yes, Ma'am. I'm your guy."

It was past noon. Ruby made another milkshake. She added cinnamon and a big glug of chocolate syrup. *If I keep eating* these I'll get fat, she reflected as she carried out two big glasses with straws.

Mike was sitting in the living room on the large leather sofa. "Ready for lunch I see." She handed him one glass and took hers to the chair.

"Look," he said. He still hadn't called her by name. "I want to know who you are and why you're here. I don't think that's unreasonable."

"I agree, totally. And I'm all about telling you *every*thing. Let's see, where did I leave off this morning? Oh yeah. The clown on the stage at the movie theater."

She explained the details of the Metaphysical Lottery prize, described the wizard coming to the pet store, and watched Mike's expression as she told him she'd chosen to become the Angel of Death. "I had an assistant. Buster—"

Mike interrupted. "Why?"

She looked at him. "I wanted to be the Angel of Death because I feel devastated when people's lives end for stupid reasons. But as I told you, the wizard couldn't give me that job so he made me an Angel. That's how I found you."

"Where are your big wings and your halo?"

"Angels look exactly like everyday people. Like how I look now."

"Just how many people *have* you intruded on?"

"You're the first one, Mike."

Ruby decided to *not* tell Mike that she no longer had any Angel powers. But she wondered about understanding the dogs and getting Mike to drink the first milkshake.

"Why?"

"Why what, Mike? Be specific."

Duke and Duchess watched, switching their attention from Mike to Ruby as if they understood.

"Why didn't you let me die? I *wanted* to die! Why'd you meddle and save my sorry ass? Why!" He slammed his empty glass down on the end table.

"Mon Dieu." Duchess murmured.

"Ca vas, Duch." The phrase, a remnant of Ruby's high-school French, relaxed the dog. Duchess lowered herself to the floor and put her muzzle between her paws.

Mike didn't seem to hear the exchange.

"You're kinda cute when you're mad, Mike. I'll tell you why I'm here. As an Angel, I could save your sorry ass for that day. But then the next day, I'd read in the morning paper that you tried to fix your life by ending it. I'd know I failed you. Miserably. I don't want to live with that. So it's for me as well as for you."

"That's a pretty tale, Ruby, but you're going to lose this battle. I'm not buying your noble reason and I don't understand what you think you're going to get out of this." Mike's snarl softened. "You might as well pack up your panties and leave."

She turned and gazed out the window. *He called me by my name.* The sun shone on the shiny leaves of a scrub oak. A fat bumblebee lumbered by.

"Truthfully, Mike, I didn't come for the antagonism although it's fun sparring with you. I didn't come because I'm attracted to you. I have a perfectly fine life waiting for me, when I'm just plain Ruby." She crossed her fingers as she said this white lie.

"So I'm made to endure your nosey interference because you want a challenge."

Ruby looked into his eyes. "I hadn't thought of that, but maybe ten percent. When I stepped in here yesterday and saw you on death's doorstep, I felt such a deep connection, I was shaking. When I came back this morning, the feeling that you and I shared something from a different lifetime was even stronger. I *do* know I owe both of us my fiercest fight to save you from destroying yourself. If you win, Mike, we both lose. If I win, we both win. Hopefully, we won't need to ride this unmerry-go-round again."

# Chapter 9

"What do you mean, *again?*"

Ruby picked up the empty glasses and started for the kitchen.

"Exactly what it sounds like, Mike. Maybe this isn't our first horror show."

"I don't know what you're talking about, but what if I call the police and have you evicted?"

"I'll tell them I'm your sis and you're mentally ill."

Mike winced.

"Have you looked at yourself in a mirror lately? You're young, but you aren't exactly a normal, healthy-looking man. Your neck doesn't look strong enough to hold up your head. The last time anyone saw you on the nightly news, a month ago, you were the picture of vitality and handsome as a movie star with your curly hair and sexy smile. Every woman in Denver lusted after you, including me. What happened, Mike?"

"None of your business. Leave or I'll . . ."

"Tell you what. When you find good homes for Duke and Duchess and you're strong enough to man-handle me out the door, I'll leave."

"You think you hold all the cards in this stupid game, don't you?"

"Not a game to me, Mike. Now, I'm going to make a pie. Do you want apple, pecan, or peach?"

He frowned. "You can *make* a pie?"

"How hard could it be? I'll Google the recipe, order the ingredients, and we'll eat it for dinner. So which kind do you want?"

Mike pushed himself up from the couch. "I don't care. I won't eat it anyhow."

"Okay. I'll make an apple pie for me and a stick-in-the-mud pie for you."

He walked out of the room. His bedroom door slammed.

Ruby washed the glasses and looked for a pie-sized baking dish. She added it to the grocery list and called Ralph's with her order.

Whistling an old tune, she assembled the ingredients for butternut squash soup.

The vegetables simmered in butter, filling the kitchen with the homey aroma of garlic and onion. She poured the chicken stock onto the vegetables, turned the fire down, and put a lid on the heavy pot.

The horseshoe knocker on the front door banged, and Pete delivered her order.

"I'll mark my calendar for every delivery you make Pete, and at number four, I'll spot you a twenty. Alright?"

"Sure, Miss Ruby," he said with a toothy grin. "That'll be great."

Eight large Pippin apples. Peel, core, and slice. The recipe made it sound so simple. An hour and a half later, she was still peeling, coring, and slicing. Crap! She finally unrolled the pre-made crust, dumped in sugary, spiced apples, dotted the mixture with butter, and tucked everything under the top crust. The recipe said to slice the top crust into strips and lattice them. *You've got to be kidding. Who am I trying to impress?*

She slid the pie into the oven. The way to a man's heart . . . if he even *has* a heart.

The soup was done. She seasoned it and let it cool. In an hour the pie would be golden brown according to the recipe. Ruby set her phone alarm and after scooping kibble into the dog dishes, went to her bedroom for a nap.

Two hours later, in a wooded glen, engaging in a steamy sexual liaison with an unrecognized man, a loud, insistent alarm blasted Ruby out of her dream. She sat up, looked for her phone, and ran to the kitchen. Smoke was seeping from the oven door. The smoke alarm was having a fit. She punched the clear button on the stove.

Mike hustled in, barefoot. The longish curls on the side of his head stuck out. "Fuck, woman! Are you trying to burn my house down?" he yelled.

She glowered at him and disconnected the smoke alarm.

"I'll thank you not to *yell* at me!" She pulled the blackened pie from the oven and set its smoking remains on the stovetop. "Four hours of work. I set my phone alarm but I left it here on the counter. It was going to be beautiful."

"You're not going to cry, are you?"

Ruby pulled the stool out from the island counter, sat, and lowered her head onto her arms.

# Chapter 10

Ruby served the Butternut squash soup to Mike in a large mug.

"What's this?"

She rolled her eyes at his look of skepticism. "It's homemade soup. The one thing I did today that turned out right."

She stood empty-handed.

"Where's yours?"

"I'm taking a time-out. It's better that I don't inflict my crummy, sad-sack mood on you or the dogs. It's been a lousy day. I'll take a nap. Do you have any sleep aids I can take?"

"Never take them."

"Aspirin?"

"Sure. Medicine cabinet in my bathroom. Help yourself while I try to get this soup down."

"Knock yourself out, Mike, and thanks for the compliment."

"Now who's being sarcastic," she heard as she turned down the hall.

"See how *you* like it," she muttered to herself.

Ruby didn't really want any aspirin. She'd wanted to see the contents of his medicine cabinet since she'd arrived.

The bathroom surprised her. A sumptuous shower with two ceiling-to-floor glass walls looked onto manzanita and scrub oak. She watched a brilliant cardinal fly to the top of a tree, cock his head, and flit away. The floor was terracotta tile and the counter was lined with colorful Mexican tiles. There were two sheepskin rugs on the floor and a large oval ceramic sink that matched the tiles.

"Wow," Ruby said. The mirrored cabinet over the sink was sparsely filled with Band-Aids, aspirin, nasal spray, and a tube of toothpaste.

No prescription bottles, no razor blades, no life-ending pills. She reached for the aspirin as Mike entered the room behind her.

"Find what you want?" he asked.

"Yes, thank you. This is a beautiful bathroom, Mike. I've been admiring it."

"Thanks. I chose everything myself."

"Ruby, I'm sorry you had a shitty day. Would you like to play a game of chess with me? Something to take your mind off your . . . crummy mood?"

She looked at him, hoping her shock didn't show.

"You *do* play chess, don't you?"

"I do, but it's been a while since I had anyone to play with. I love the game . . . I've missed it."

"Go take your aspirin. I'll bring in the set."

Ruby stumbled from the room. Don't think that this kindness will last, she told herself. But . . . what a surprise. He has empathy after all. Why did I assume . . .

In the kitchen, she faked taking the aspirin in case he came in. Mike sat on the sofa with the chess set assembled on the coffee table and an easy chair pulled up to the opposite side. He'd given her the white set.

"I'm rusty. Go through how the different pieces can move, please. It will all come back to me, then."

He started with the king and went through the ranks, ending with the pawns. "Got it?" he asked.

"I think so. But don't expect any brilliance until the second game, Mike." She smiled as she said this. "You move first, okay?"

"No, the first move is important. We'll flip a coin. Do you have one?"

"I don't. As a matter of fact, I don't even own a purse. Or a bank account. I'm literally penniless."

Mike stared at her. "Why? Didn't you have a job before you came here?"

"Remember I told you how I became an Angel? Before that, I worked at Pet City. I don't pretend to know how the wizard did this, but when he whisked me away from the chore I was doing at the store, I looked back, and there was another Ruby, basically me, scooping the dog poo I'd been scooping a second before." She watched Mike's face.

"She became the other me, doing my job, collecting my paychecks, and spending my bank account. Sounds bizarre, I know, but it's what happened. She even inherited my boyfriend."

"Say I believe all this," he leaned back and closed his eyes, "there's two of you now?"

"I can hardly believe it myself, and I lived every second of it. To answer your question, no. There aren't two of us. I look completely different now. *Really* different. All the metaphysical doing of the wizard."

"Did this wizard pay you?"

"I broke my contract. I didn't complete the fourteen days so I got zip."

"You couldn't take it anymore? That's why you broke the contract?"

She was quiet. Mike leaned forward.

"I broke the contract to come here and convince you that life," she paused, "is precious."

The conversation stalled. They sat and looked at each other.

"Did you ever do something that you knew, win, lose, or draw, you *had* to do?" She hadn't dropped her gaze and neither had Mike. "That's why I . . ."

"Damn you," Mike finally said.

A tiny smile curled the corners of Ruby's lips. "Damn *you*."

They played the game. Mike didn't show any mercy, and Ruby fumbled along, slowly remembering after each attack on her key pieces, what she'd done wrong.

"Well, that was a complete disaster. It's coming back to me, though. I'll do better next time."

"There's not going to be a next time," Mike said.

Ruby felt stung. "That's mean! I told you I hadn't played in a long time. Don't be a jerk!" Tears stung her eyes. "I thought this game was to take my mind off the crummy day I've had. You just set me up to fail so you can kick me while I'm . . ."

"So now you're pulling the crying act on me. Is it your time of the month, Ruby?"

Ruby's eyes widened. "I *cannot* believe you said that, Michael Harrington!"

As she stood, she flipped the chess board scattering the remaining pieces to the floor. "You can shove your precious game where the sun doesn't shine, you— you . . . cretin!" Ruby glared at him and turned to stomp out of the room.

"Wait," Mike said softly.

"Hell, no! I've had enough!" She turned and looked hard at him. "Do you have a gunny sack or something I can throw my stuff in? I'll get out of your hair, and by the way, if you don't croak, you should get a haircut!"

There was a long silence. Mike closed his eyes. Ruby looked hard at his face but could read nothing in his expression.

"Well?" Ruby finally said. "I need something I can drag down the road behind me."

"Ruby, I apologize. I don't want you to leave. I, I'm sorry for . . . everything. Please. Forgive me. I'll even get a haircut. Okay?"

"Why?" she said. "Why should I stay? You've made it perfectly clear that you don't want me here."

Mike covered his eyes with one bony hand. "Having you here, being so positive, taking every nasty thing I threw at you . . . I, I just realized that . . . well, don't leave, Ruby. Please," he whispered.

Ruby sat down on the sofa, buffeted by Mike's mood change.

"If I stay . . ."

"If you stay, things will be different."

# Chapter 11

Mike and Ruby sat, looking at each other. Duke and Duchess, lying side by side on the Navajo rug, seemed to have followed the conversation.

"How different?" Ruby finally asked. Her blue eyes bored into his.

"I don't know, but I'm going to try."

"Huh. Okay Mike, I have an idea. Let's take these stinky dogs to the groomers and get them shampooed and clipped. I'll bet they haven't been bathed in more than a month."

He looked at them. "They need their nails trimmed too."

Ruby covered her surprise. "You're right. Besides, they're almost out of kibble."

On cue, the large, black poodles rose and pirouetted in a happy dance.

"You take them," Mike said in a flat voice.

Her eyebrows shot up. "Why? They're *your* dogs. I can't handle two large dogs by myself. What if they see a cat? What if one slips out of my grip? You owe them your care, Mike."

"The groomer probably can't take them today."

"Call and find out. If not today, we'll go tomorrow."

"I don't want to see her," he mumbled.

Oh, it's like that, Ruby thought.

"Girlfriend?"

"No. Just a nice woman I've known for a while. She loves the dogs."

"So Mike, if she's special, maybe she *should* know you've been going through a rough patch. If it's just vanity, it's not worthy of you."

It got quiet. The dogs settled down. Duke put his muzzle between his front paws. His eyes beneath the black curly mop switched from his master to the lady who talked his language.

"Tell him, Duke. Tell Mike you love him and you want him to take you."

Duke rose majestically as only a blue-ribbon standard poodle can, walked to Mike, and put his paw on the man's knee. Duke's long red tongue delicately slid up Mike's neck to end at the top of his ear.

"Good boy, Duke."

Mike stared at Duke. Then, at Ruby. "How did you . . . "

She smiled. "How did I what? Shall I get you the phone?"

A quiet minute ticked by.

"Gr-r-r-r," Mike growled.

She handed him the phone wearing a big smile. "You're funny."

He sighed, thumbed his contacts, and as the groomer's phone rang, said, "She won't have an opening today. Maybe not even tomo— oh, hello Cathy. Mike Harrington here."

He turned on the speaker. "Listen to this."

"Mike! Where have you been? I decided you were two-timing me with another groomer. How the hell are you?"

"I . . . , I haven't been well." He moved on. "The dogs need the works. When can you fit them in?"

"Can you get them here at four-thirty? I have two cancelations so you can fill those slots. I've missed you, Mikey.

Maybe we can have a beer afterward. Sit around in the back room and tell each other lies."

"We'll play it by ear, Cathy. See you at four-thirty." He thumbed to end the call.

"That worked out well," Ruby enthused. "She sounds fun and she certainly likes you."

"She's not my type. It takes thirty minutes to get there so we need to leave ten minutes ago."

"I'm ready."

He looked at her boot-cut Levis and bright-red western snap shirt that showed off her curves.

"Get your wallet and keys," Ruby said. "I'll get the leashes. We'll meet you in the garage."

The car, she observed, was a midnight-blue BMW X3 sport-utility. The dogs ran to the back, watching the tailgate eagerly. Mike remoted it open and the dogs leaped in and settled down in their travel pen. He pushed the start button and the engine fired off quietly as the tailgate slid closed and the garage door rose.

"Nice car," she said as they backed out of the garage into the circular drive.

"My God, it's bright out here," he said. "Sunglasses in the glove box." He pointed.

"Say the magic word."

"You're a pain in the butt."

"Nope. Wrong words. Look, Mike, even if you *were* paying me, which you aren't, you'd still owe me common courtesy. I'm sure your mommy taught you that."

"Paying you for what?" he said as he eased into a busy street. "Moving into my house? Bossing me around? I . . ." he looked sheepish and then motioned zipping his lips.

Ruby reached into the glove box and extracted a pair of gold-rimmed aviators. She held them up, out of reach.

"Well, let's see. Cooking, cleaning, ordering groceries, doing laundry, feeding the dogs, and keeping you from dying prematurely by your own manly hands. All I'm asking for in return is one nice word." She put on the glasses and smiled at him.

"Okay. May I puleeeze have my sunglasses?"

"Prettily said." She cleaned them on her shirt tail and handed them over.

They were quiet for the rest of the way to the groomers. Ruby glanced at him. He seemed relaxed, enjoying being out of the house, driving expertly in the busy city. She mentally patted herself on the back.

He pulled into a small storefront in a strip mall. The sign said Cathy's Pet Spa. Mike let the dogs out of the back and the four trooped in.

Cathy came out of the back with a big smile.

"Mike, you look lousy! What the hell happened?"

They hugged. She was stocky but tiny, only coming up to his shirt pockets. Her honey-blond hair was pulled into a ponytail and her brown knit polo and crepe-soled shoes reminded Ruby of her Pet City days. Cathy's brown eyes assessed her. She stepped up with an offered handshake.

"Hi, I'm Cathy. What have you done to my friend?"

"I'm Ruby Louise. I found him this way."

A young man came out of the back. "Are these guys our 4:30s?"

"Yeah. Get them started and I'll be right back. Are you going to hang out, Mike?"

"No. We need to get dog food. What time should we be back?"

"Should be done by six. Shampoo, cut and toenails?"

"That's it. If we get something to eat, can we bring something back for you?"

"Just your scrawny self. Get out of here so I can get to work."

Mike and Ruby got into the BMW. "She's cute," Ruby said. "A diamond in the rough."

"Yeah." He backed out and pulled into traffic. "Let's get the dog food first. I'm hungry for a hamburger. I know a place."

"God, that sounds good," she said to cover her surprise. "I'd love a hamburger."

They drove to Pet City. "Mike, this is where I worked before I became an Angel."

In the store, she looked around. "See that man over there? He's Mr. Boone, the manager."

She looked at Mike. "This is crazy. Here he comes."

Mr. Boone strolled over. His eyes slid from Ruby's face to her cleavage peeking from the top snap of her red shirt.

"Hello, folks. How can I direct you?" His eyes finally drifted up to hers.

"We're looking for the Premier Organic dog food," Ruby said. "The fifty-pound size." She tipped her head, squinted at his hairpiece, and frowned.

Flustered, he scurried to the checkout counter, patting his head. He picked up a small round mic and said in an imperious voice, "Lizzie, bring a fifty of Premier to the front."

"Mike," she whispered, as Mr. Boone hurried off. "This was my job before I became an Angel."

A huge bag of kibble, two arms, and two chino-clad legs appeared. Mike stepped forward and took it from her. Ruby did a double take. The woman's straight brown hair was parted in the middle and held back by barrettes at her temples. Ruby

Louise had never worn her hair that way because she hated the freckles that make-up couldn't hide.

The two women stared at each other.

"Lizzie, did something really strange happen to you?"

Lizzie's eyes got big. "You know about the wizard?"

"Oh my, yes. We were both offered an opportunity by the wizard. Do you like your new life?"

"Do I! I love my new life."

Mike left the checkout stand with the dog food.

"I'm happy for you, Liz." She turned and ran to open the door for Mike.

In the car, they looked at each other.

"Wow, wow, wow, Mike."

Her eyes glistened with tears.

"Are you okay?"

"I'll be okay . . . I just need . . . a good hamburger."

# Chapter 12

The encounter in the pet store where she'd worked only a week ago was a jolt. Liz seemed happy with her new life. Ruby wasn't sure about her own new life.

Mike pulled into a small hole-in-the-wall lunch place called Mom and Pop's.

"Best hamburgers in Denver," Mike proclaimed

"I'm salivating," she said.

He looked at her and grinned. Ruby's heart fluttered. Damn, he's cute when he's . . . cute. If he starts eating real food, he'll fill out the deep blue flannel shirt and perfectly faded Levi's he's wearing. He needs a haircut. Another outing soon, she thought. They stepped into the tiny lunch stop.

Red-painted tables for two and four lined the wall. The order counter, menu board, and kitchen were on the other side of the room. A comfortably filled-out woman behind the counter smiled at them. A grandma, Ruby decided . . . probably gives great hugs. She admired her white hair, tied back in an old-fashioned red bandana setting off her soft, unblemished complexion. Ruby wanted to adopt her.

It was late for lunch and early for closing, so only two boot-clad men sat at one of the tables.

Mike knew what he wanted. "Two cheeseburgers with everything, two slaws, one order of French fries, and a chocolate shake with two glasses." He turned to her. "Alright with you?"

"Perfect." She heard two patties hit the grill through the opening under the menu board. Pop, wearing a tall chef's hat and a white apron, waved at her with an industrial-sized spatula. Ruby waved back. She grinned when his hat slid down over one eye.

The smell of the cooking meat almost brought tears to her eyes. *Maybe my emotional rush is about seeing Mike enthused about food.*

They chose the corner table and sat across from each other. Mike checked his watch. "We have forty-five minutes to eat and get back to Cathy's. We'll make it."

Mike jumped up and brought the food as soon as it was ready. It took up almost every inch of the table. They picked up their burgers and took the first bite.

"M-m-m-m," she moaned. The bun had been lightly toasted. It tasted homemade, yeasty. Spicy mustard, tomato, thin-sliced crisp onion, lettuce and, the juiciest meat ever.

"This place should be written up in the *Where to Dine* section of the Post."

She took a sip of the milkshake. "Homemade ice cream? I've died and gone to Heaven, Mike."

Big grin as he chewed. They'd both been on a liquid diet. Even the main course was too much for their shrunken stomachs.

"I thought I was so hungry."

"Me too. We can box it up and finish it at home." That didn't sound right. "I mean at *your* home," she amended.

Mike gave her a funny look she didn't know how to interpret.

They pulled up to the dog spa and went in. Cathy brought Duke and Duchess out. Duke wore a red bow-tie ribbon.

Duchess wore a pink bow in her pompadour. They were sparkly clean, sculpted, and combed. Their trimmed toenails gleamed.

"Get us out of this dorky stuff, lady. We hate it," Duke growled. "We stink," Duchess whined. "Maybe we can roll in something good at home."

"Excellent work, Cathy," Ruby gushed.

"Yeah. Next time don't wait so long, Mike. Took extra work." She turned to Ruby. "You going to take them for a walk so Mikey and I can catch up?"

He was in full view of Cathy so he couldn't signal a message.

"I can't handle two large dogs by myself." She searched Mike's eyes. If he argues, I'll back down.

"She's right", he said. "They might be too much of a handful. Rain check on the beer, Cathy." He paid with his credit card and slid a twenty as a tip. "Put me down for a month."

"Three weeks," Cathy said. "I'll call." She glared at Ruby and stuffed the bill in her pocket.

"Thanks, Cathy," Mike said. "Come on crew. Let's go home."

As they walked to the door, Mike casually put his arm around Ruby's shoulders as if he'd done it many times.

Outside, she said, "Think she got it?"

He looked down at her. "Yeah. Thanks for going along."

"You're welcome . . . I kind of liked it."

She climbed into the passenger seat. Mike took the dogs to the back and opened the hatch.

Ruby put the visor down and caught Mike's face in the vanity mirror.

His grin matched hers.

# Chapter 13

"Mike Dear."

Mike looked up and attempted to read Ruby's expression.

"Oh-Oh. When you start a sentence like that, I know I'm not going to like it."

Ruby was quiet while he marked his place and closed the book.

"We've been together for three months now, and I've been offered a special project. I'm going to say yes."

He sighed. "What kind of offer and by whom?"

"I've been speaking to Abdul. There's a situation happening in Heaven that's affecting the entire world. He asked me if I wanted to go there undercover to help deal with it."

Mike stared at her. Two furrows appeared between his brows. He ran his hand through curls that were overdue for another trim.

"Ruby, in spite of a rocky start, I've gotten fond of you. If you . . . care about me, get this idea right out of your mind. And who the hell is this Abdul? You know, all those psychedelic drugs you did in your youth left you a little . . . "

"For your information, Michael Harrington," she interrupted, "I was a goodie-two-shoes! Abdul was my metaphysical advisor when I—" she stopped. "Oh, never mind. You don't believe anything about how I became an Angel."

He sighed. "So you're going to Heaven to deal with a worldwide situation," he said, his voice heavy with innuendo. "Isn't death a requirement? The last time I looked, you're alive."

"Of course, I'll go to Heaven alive. Abdul will bring me back when I'm done. Not to worry, Mike."

"NOT TO WORRY! Tell Mr. Crack-Pot to go straight to hell. Better yet, tell him to go fix Heaven himself. I don't like the fairy tale this Abdul character wants you to believe, Ruby. Not one bit!"

She sat down next to Mike on the sofa. With her head on his shoulder, she stroked his thigh.

"Mike darling, I love you too, but when we talked about our growing affection, we promised we wouldn't try to control each other. Remember?"

"Yes, but this is out of the question, dammit! Even if you going to Heaven *is* possible, it would undo me."

She sat, eyes unfocused, while she sought a route to Mike's understanding.

Duke, ignoring the conflict, lay chewing a rawhide the size of an arm bone. Duchess listened to the conversation. She walked over to Ruby and laid her long, black muzzle on her knee. *Offer him a bone.*

Ruby frowned. *He's not fond of bones*, she told Duchess.

*Not a meat bone*, Duchess said. She looked into Ruby's eyes, and said, *you know.*

*Not that kind of bone. Okay, Sex? That's already our recreation of choice. Hmm. He hasn't started back to work yet. He sits around the house, bored.*

"Mike, my time on this Heaven project would go faster if you went with me. Be my assistant. My Watson, so to speak."

"Watson! I remember the old Basil Rathbone shows. Watson was a bumbling fool who got everything wrong."

"Okay, I didn't mean like that. I meant we could sleuth together and be twice as effective at getting to the problem. And twice as fast at fixing it. Two brains instead of one. Like Brad and Angelina in Mr. and Mrs. Smith. Oh, wait. Not a good example."

"We assassinate each other? So that's how we die? What the *hell*, Ruby!"

"Stop focusing on the death part. We don't die. Abdul sends us to Heaven disguised as a dearly departed couple and when we're done, he brings us back, good as new. Doesn't that sound more interesting than moping around the house?"

"And meanwhile, what happens to Duke and Duchess?"

"The story will be that we all perished together in your Cessna. They'd go with us."

Long silence. *Is he considering the idea?* She watched Mike lean back, close his eyes, and crack his knuckles.

"Here's my challenge, Mr. Skeptical. I'll call Abdul and invite him to come and answer all your questions. If you're not convinced that everything I've told you about my metaphysical experience was true, I'll go to Heaven by myself. But if you are convinced, you and the dogs go too. Deal?"

"So, heads you win, tails I lose. Call Abdul. But NO deal."

Ruby picked up her phone and punched in the number.

"Abdul, Mike and I are discussing the Heaven project. Could you come over and clear up some questions for us?"

Immediately, the door knocker sounded. Mike stood and accompanied the dogs to the door. He opened it to see a tall, skinny man, holding a scruffy NY Yankees baseball cap. His short beard, curly hair, and his eyes were coal black.

"Hi. I'm Abdul."

Abdul ... ? Mike was expecting someone celestial, not this ... street person. After a tiny pause, Mike invited him in.

He watched Abdul wipe his shabby Adidases on the mat and stroll regally into the terracotta-tiled entrance.

"Were you already waiting outside?"

Before Abdul could answer, Ruby appeared and ushered him into the great room. Duchess pranced beside him. Duke returned to his rawhide chew.

"So good to see you, Abdul." She introduced him to Mike, who put his hand out.

"Oh, Abdul doesn't shake hands, Mike. Temporal differences, you know."

"Oh, sorry," Mike said. "Uh, can I get you something to drink?"

"Mint tea, if you have it."

"I'll see if I can stir some up." He glanced at Ruby.

"Hot, with lots of sugar and fresh mint leaves, Darling. I'll have one too."

With Mike out of the room, Ruby grinned at her friend. She gestured to a chair. He sat and smiled a snaggle-tooth grin at her.

"Abdul, I'm excited about this Heaven project but Mike doesn't believe I was an Angel or that you can send me to Heaven and bring me back alive. He's sure I'm a bit mad. I'm trying to talk him into going with me."

The tea kettle whistled in the kitchen.

"What can *I* do, Miss Ruby?"

"Can you convince him we can do this? Nothing I've said has worked."

A smile spread across Abdul's face.

# Chapter 14

Mike came into the room carrying a tray with three mugs of tea. A terrible shriek cut through the air. Mike slammed the tray onto the coffee table, sloshing the tea and overturning the sugar.

All their eyes were on Duke who had rolled to his side, open mouth silent as his chest convulsed.

Mike ran to him, running his finger into the gaping mouth.

"He's choking!" He looked at Ruby and Abdul, standing behind him. "Ruby! Do something!" Mike yelled. "He's not breathing."

Abdul nodded to Ruby. In a trance, she stepped around Mike, pointed her finger over the prone dog, and circled her arm. They heard a snap. She sat down heavily and held her head.

Duke struggled to his feet. After five painful hacks, he heaved up a tangled lump of shredded rawhide. He wobbled into the kitchen. They heard him lapping water from his dish.

Mike rose and looked at Abdul and Ruby. "You two set this up to show me, didn't you?"

Her eyes blazed. "*You* bought that awful rawhide bone at Pet City. *You* gave it to him this morning. Abdul granted me the power to step in. I saved Duke's life and all you can think is it's our fault that Duke almost choked to death. The next thing out of your mouth better be an apology, Mike Harrington!"

Mike put up his hands. "I'm sorry."

"Let's sit and start this conversation from the beginning," Abdul proposed. "Do you have any questions, Mike?"

"Do you mind if I throw this rawhide away and clean up the mess?"

"That's your question?"

"I have another. Shall I make more tea?"

Ruby smiled. "That would be appreciated, Mike."

With Mike out of the room, she looked at Abdul. "*Did* you set that up?"

"Of course . . . not."

Mike came back with a steaming pot of tea. They all sugared their mugs, and Ruby poured.

"Duke seems okay, but I'm still shaking," Mike told them. They sipped their tea for a quiet moment.

"Abdul, tell me about this Heaven thing. Ruby thinks the dogs and I should go too. I'm concerned about the dying and then being restored to life."

"Start with what you call the dying," Abdul said.

"Okay. Will it be painful? Will we leave our bloody bodies here for the cleaning lady to find? Will there be funerals and news coverage? You know, I'm known in Denver. This won't go unnoticed. Then when we come back . . . presumably alive, what's our story? There'll be reporters. How do we explain where we've been and why we're alive?"

"All perfectly understandable concerns, Mike. I like the idea of your entire family going on this mission. Four brains are better than one. No, there will be no pain and there will be no bloody bodies. This isn't death. You will simply go to sleep at night and wake up in Heaven. An Angel will greet you and escort you to where you will stay."

"Whoa, Abdul! Will we still be us or wispy fragments? Can we talk? Will we be like the . . . inhabitants or will we stick out as foreigners? I don't wear pajamas. Will I be naked?"

Abdul stirred his mint tea, took a sip, and set the mug on the table. "No need to overthink things, Mike. You'll find out everything easily when you get there. Just relax and enjoy acquainting yourselves with everyone in beautiful Heaven."

"Huh," Mike scratched his head. "Okay, what if this takes months or years to deal with? How will our extended disappearances be explained?"

"Time in Heaven is different from time in this reality, Mike. No matter how long it takes, you'll be home tomorrow for breakfast."

"Really!" Ruby was as surprised as Mike. She smiled at him over the rim of her mug.

"Okay, Abdul. Here's the big question. What's the problem we're going up to assess?"

"Before I tell you, Mike, are you going with Miss Ruby?"

Abdul sat relaxed, one leg resting on his other knee, sipping his tea. His jeans were frayed at the hem. His long-sleeved shirt had seen the inside of a washing machine too many times.

"Abdul," Mike said, "Why don't *you* go to Heaven and fix whatever's wrong?"

"Good question. I'm too well-known. I'd have no power. Politics, you know."

"There's *politics* in Heaven?"

"Of course. There's a congress who interprets the will of all the souls."

"Well I'll be damned," Mike said. He sat thinking. "Okay, what exactly is the problem?"

"It seems nobody in Heaven wants to be reborn to Earth. The world population is decreasing . . . alarmingly. Heaven is limitless but it's causing a tremendous imbalance."

Mike blinked, staring at Abdul. "And you think the two of us can turn it around?"

"The thing is, you two have the advantage of being of this reality. Don't let them indoctrinate you. If I wasn't sure of your success, Mike, I wouldn't promote this."

It was quiet as they sipped their tea. Duke came back into the room and settled down at Mike's feet.

"I have a question," Ruby said. "When we want to come back, do I click my heels together three times and say there's no place like home?"

Abdul smiled. "That's as good as anything. So are you in?"

"Of course I'm going. I want to see what Heaven's like." She looked at Mike. "Are you going, love?" Her voice was quiet.

"Hell, no. Sorry. You'll only be gone for a day. I'll stay here with the dogs."

She set her tea down and slumped. Her eyes wandered to Abdul's. He didn't seem disappointed.

"When's the departure?" Mike asked. "Next week?"

"You'll wake up in Heaven tomorrow," Abdul said. "Buster will be your guide."

"Buster? The dog?"

# Chapter 15

Mike climbed into bed. Ruby, already under the covers, snuggled with him.

"Ruby, what are you thinking? You can't wear that to Heaven."

"What do you want me to wear?"

"Uh, jeans and a sweatshirt. It might be chilly. You hate to be cold. And take your toothbrush."

"But I have an electric toothbrush. Do you think there's electricity in Heaven?"

They were quiet, contemplating what they didn't know about Ruby's trip.

"We're overthinking this, Mike. Nothing bad happens in Heaven. It's Heavenly, right?"

"Who says? You haven't talked to anyone who could tell you what goes on in Heaven, right? Nobody dies, goes to this mythical Heaven, and comes back to tell us about it. Does that tell you something?"

No answer.

"Are you asleep?"

"No, Mike. I'm thinking. So you think Abdul is going to let me wake up someplace weird, unprepared, and not in this life? He wouldn't put me in a dangerous or uncomfortable situation. Remember, all I need to do when I want to come home is click my heels together. Besides, Buster's going to be there. Buster's no bullshit."

"Somehow, Ruby, I don't find that reassuring. It's not too late to change your mind."

"I told Abdul I'm going and I'm going. Now let's go to sleep and see what happens in the morning."

"What happens if I don't go to sleep?" he said.

"I don't know. Why don't you try it? Goodnight, Mike."

As soon as she heard Mike's soft snores, she closed her eyes and drifted off.

"Mike?"

"What?"

"Are you asleep?"

After a pause, he answered. "I'm awake. I never went to sleep."

"You were snoring."

"I was faking so you'd go to sleep. Why'd you wake me up?"

"What do you think they wear in Heaven?"

"I don't know. Probably not jeans and sweatshirts. Maybe they go naked. That way, they wouldn't need washing machines and laundromats. Why are you worrying about that? Just go to sleep, you'll find out everything in the morning."

"So you think Heaven is a huge nudist colony? No. I don't want to see everybody's naked body. What if I run into my Uncle Charley? Yuck!"

It was quiet until she heard Mike's soft snores again.

"Mike," she whispered. "Are you faking again?"

No answer. To get the image of a Heaven full of naked uncles out of her head, Ruby slowly counted down from one hundred. She got to seventy-nine. When she opened her eyes again, light was seeping from edges of the window.

"It's about time you woke up," Buster said. He was sitting on the foot of the bed.

Mike's eyes opened. "I remember you. What are you doing in our bedroom?"

"You're in Heaven, Dopey," Buster said. "Did you think you'd wake up on a cloud?"

"You *talk?* Oh, great! I thought Ruby was going to be met by an Angel. Wait! *I'm* in Heaven? What the hell! I'm not going to Heaven. There's been a horrible mistake! Send me back! Right now! I mean it, Buster."

"No mistake," Buster said. "Now get up. We have an appointment to keep."

"Buster, take me to the head honcho. I'm *not* staying here!"

Buster jumped off the bed. "Just follow me. Everything's ready for you." He stood at the door and looked back at them.

Mike threw back the quilt and marched to the bathroom door where his robe hung. Ruby put on the Adidases she'd left by the bed. They met at the door. Mike put his hand on the knob but didn't turn it.

"C'mon! Let's get this show on the road," Buster growled.

"Wait! We have to get the dogs. Where are they?"

"They've been out for hours. They're playing with all the other dogs. Don't worry. It's a dog park out there."

Mike turned the doorknob and slowly opened the door. Buster ran out, but Mike and Ruby stood in the doorway and stared.

Green grass grew as far as they could see. Duel paths stretched across the gently rolling landscape. On one path, were ordinary-looking people on bicycles, tricycles, scooters, roller skates, and skateboards. No one was naked, Ruby noted. On the second path, people walked, many hand-in-hand. Shade trees dotted the land. Other areas seemed to be verdant woods.

"It looks . . . rather uh, mundane," Ruby said under her breath.

Buster nudged her calf. "They're waiting for you. We'll show you everything later. Follow me."

"Wait," Mike protested. "I need to see my dogs."

"Just whistle, Mike," Buster said. "They'll come."

He gave a loud whistle. Duke and Duchess ran up, their tongues hanging out.

"Hi, Dad," Duke panted. "Whatcha want?"

"We're playing with some Irish Setters," Duchess panted. "This place is fun!"

Mike's eyes got big. "You can . . . talk!" he sputtered.

"We could always talk after we grew up, Dad. You just couldn't understand us," Duke said. "Can we go play now?"

"Uh, okay. Just stay close enough to hear my whistle."

They galloped off. Mike turned to Ruby. "Did you hear them too?"

"I always hear them, Mike. From my Angel days. Cool, huh?"

"Mike? Ruby?" They turned to see a beautiful woman in a fuchsia gown, speaking to them.

"My name's Alice. Please follow me." She turned and walked down a path toward a cottage. Her apple-green hair hung down her back in two thick braids. They glistened in the sunlight.

Ruby and Mike glanced at each other. "Here we go," Ruby whispered. "Down the rabbit hole."

The cottage had stone walls and a thatched roof. Alice stood at the open door and beckoned them in.

"This is the garment dispensary. Pick out the colors you like in your sizes. Any questions?"

"Um, Alice, what's the fiber? I only wear cotton or linen."

"This fiber is dirt-proof, tear and wear-proof. It never wrinkles, fades or shrinks." She smiled at them. "We're a little short on stock at the moment, so please limit yourselves to three of everything. Dressing rooms are down the hall. Please leave your Earth clothes in the stall. I'll be waiting outside." She stepped out and closed the door.

"Must be plastic," Mike said. "I'll just wear my robe. I'm going home as soon as I can see the Angel-in-Charge."

"Mikey, you can't wear your robe. You'll blow my cover. This fabric doesn't feel like plastic." She fingered a tunic top. "It feels like silk and cotton. I like it."

"I'm not gonna wear these," Mike held up the drawstring pants. They were soft and loose with a slight flair. "I'd look like a hippie."

Ruby held up a pair in lavender. "The styles are all the same. Just different colors. I like them. Those hippies knew what they were doing." She added a pair in yellow and another in sky blue. She chose matching tops.

"Wear the gowns, Mike. You'll look like one of the disciples." She added a gown to her choices. "I'm going to change. Maybe, when we look like everybody else, we can get some coffee."

"Or I can demand to see the head Guru." He pulled a beige set from the men's section.

She left him to grapple with his dilemma, and stepped into a changing room, smiling.

# Chapter 16

Mike walked out of the dressing room wearing wheat-colored pants and a tunic.

"You look very manly," Ruby told him.

"There's no underwear."

"I know. I guess in Heaven we don't need underwear."

"I don't like it. I feel exposed."

She looked. "You're perfectly covered up."

"I am now, but what if . . . ?"

"Look in the mirror, Mike. The tunics are long for a reason. You'll get used to it. I'm not wearing a bra. I like it. Let's go see what's next. Okay?"

Ruby opened the door and stepped out. Mike reluctantly followed.

Alice and Buster were sitting on a bench under a shade tree, talking. Alice glanced up. "Oh, shoes. Mike, looks like you wear elevens and Ruby, what? Six?"

"Right on both. Do we get to choose a color?"

"Wait here. I think you'll like these." She went into the cottage and came out with two pairs of grey, woven, soft-soled slip-ons. Ruby took off her Adidases and pulled on the shoes. They immediately changed to the exact shade of lavender of her clothes. Mike saw the same thing happen when he pulled his on.

"These are great. Do they come in espadrilles?"

Mike walked around like he was in a shoe store. "Perfect for strolling, but what if I want to dig a hole, or do a little rock climbing?"

"Just one style, but you'll find these adequate for any activity, my dears," Alice said. "And now, let's get you indoctrinated. Come with me."

They exchanged looks.

"Alice," Mike said. "I'd like to see the person in charge, please."

"Right away, Michael, after you're indoctrinated."

"We'd like to walk around with Buster first," Ruby said. "We want to see where we're going to live and talk to some of the folks here. There'll be plenty of time later."

Alice looked quizzical. "Okay," she said.

Buster jumped down from the bench. They strolled down the sloping hill. When they were out of Alice's hearing range, he gave them a critical look.

"You two almost fit in here. Remember, nobody gets angry in Heaven. No aggression and no confrontation. Don't walk fast. Glide along like you have all the time in the . . . Just keep a beatific expression on your faces."

"How do you know all this, Buster?"

"Because, you dufus. I'm a dog.

"Dufus! Where do you get off—"

"When I called you a dufus, Mike, I was testing you. You didn't pass the test."

"What test!" Mike snarled.

"See? Now your face is all puckered up again. People are coming toward us. If they see your face like this, they'll know you don't belong here. You don't want to get kicked out of Heaven. You wouldn't like the other place."

Mike frowned. The other place? Could Abdul do that? He wondered. A couple strolled toward them holding hands. They smiled. He smiled back.

"Nice day," the woman said.

"Beatific," Mike answered.

When they were far enough away, Mike turned to Ruby. "I want to go home!"

"Mike, Abdul tricked us and sent you here with me. But just one more of Abdul's sly tricks and I promise, when you say the word, we'll both go back to Denver. Deal?"

Mike was quiet. "I'm thinking," he finally said. "Okay, but I'll be watching."

"Me too, Mike." They strolled toward the cottages, holding hands.

"Buster, is everyone in Heaven young? Don't seniors or children come here?"

"Sure, but in Heaven, everyone's twenty-eight. It's the perfect age, you know."

"I'm twenty-eight, but that's my only qualification for this screwball place."

"Remember, Mike, you and Ruby are here undercover to reverse the imbalance. You need to fit in. I'm here to put you through Heaven boot camp."

"Great! A drill sergeant . . . dog. This keeps getting worse."

"You know, Buster," Ruby said, "We haven't had coffee yet. Can we slow down and get this off to a better start? Surely Heaven has coffee. We can't be blissful when we're grumpy."

"Caffeine, huh? Dogs don't need coffee to be blissful. Follow me. Remember, stroll like you have no worries, and aren't caffeine-deprived."

Buster demonstrated. He smelled a flower. He watched a butterfly. He stopped and lazily scratched behind one ear. He glanced back. Mike and Ruby were still standing in the same spot with mutinous looks.

"Shall I kick him in the butt or do you want to do the honors?"

"Buster, is this another stupid test? Here's a test for you; I can click my heels together and we'll be home. It will be your fault. Coffee. Now!"

"Why didn't you say? Why are you standing around jawing at me? Let's go." He dog-trotted down the path. Mike and Ruby glanced at each other and followed, greeting other strollers with smiles and little waves.

"They've all had their coffee," Mike murmured.

Buster led them to a Y in the path. One path led to a ramada. Vines grew thickly on tree-trunk uprights. A massive profusion of cascading purple blooms hung from the latticed roof.

They stared. "We're not in Denver anymore," Ruby whispered.

Three people filled mugs from spigots from a glass jug twice the size of an office water cooler. Smaller jugs dispensed cream and sugar. They watched as a young man creamed and then sugared his mug. Next, he pressed a lever, and a spoon ejected. He picked it up and stirred as he joined a group sitting at a table.

"Let's go," Mike said. "There's only one choice. We don't know if it's caf or decaf, but at this point I don't care."

They picked up mugs and filled them with steaming coffee. It smelled . . . heavenly. Ruby doctored hers while Mike took his to an empty table. Hummingbirds and butterflies flitted and hummed in and out of the fragrant blooms.

"Mike, see that table with those men and women?"

"What about them?"

"They're talking and laughing instead of looking at their phones."

"No phones in Heaven," Buster said.

"None? Zip?" Mike asked. "How do they . . . Oh. No business."

"Right. People visit when they want to talk to each other."

When Buster's charges had been properly caffeinated, he said, "Okay troops, ready to carry on? Want to see where you'll live?"

"I can hardly wait," Mike muttered.

Buster took a path that led to the top of the next hill. They met people strolling. On the sister path, a few rolled by on skates or bicycles.

At the crest of the hill, Ruby and Mike stopped. Cottages stretched as far as they could see. On the horizon, they looked like dots.

"They're all light colors. Why aren't there any dark ones, Buster?"

"No dark or strong colors in Heaven."

"I noticed, but why?"

"If I could shrug, I would. It's just the way it is."

"Wait a minute. What time is it Mike?"

He looked at his watch. "The hands and numbers are gone!"

"I forgot to tell you, Mike. There's no time here."

"Wait," Mike said. "There's no time? How do people . . . ?"

"They don't miss it. Remember, they've all died. Come on. I'll show you your cottage."

Mike shook his head. "I don't like this Ruby. So far, I don't see why anyone would want to stay in this place."

"We've only been here for . . . an hour? Let's get the dogs and see what the rest of the day is like. Maybe take a nap. Right now, I'm on overload."

He whistled and in seconds, Duke and Duchess ran up.

"You two stay with us. We're going to see where we'll live."

"Sure, Dad," Duchess panted. "We're tired, anyway."

"Buster, we don't have any money. We can't rent a cottage."

"This is Heaven, Ruby. Nobody pays for anything. It's all free. No rent, no mortgages, no cars or car repair shops, and no insurance of any kind."

She thought for a minute. "I'm beginning to see why there's a problem."

# Chapter 17

Mike and Ruby followed Buster down the hill, turned left, and walked to a path named Twenty-Ninth Row. Duke and Duchess followed, tongues hanging out.

"Rather a prosaic name for a path in Heaven isn't it?" she said.

"What would you name it?" Mike asked. "I find it quite down to Earth, myself."

"That's just it, Mike. We're not down to Earth, are we? I would name it . . . Strawberry Shortcake Way."

"Or . . . T-bone Steak Trail," Mike suggested as they strolled by cottages, distinguished from each other only by color.

"I think we're hungry. Buster, is there a café?"

"After you see your accommodations, I'll take you there. Here we are. Your bit of Heaven." He turned down the walk, thickly lined with pansies. They matched the seafoam blue of the house. The grass, shrubs, and leaves were green but every blossom was seafoam blue.

"I've never seen flowers this color, Buster."

"It's how you tell your house from the others. There's no other house on this street in this color. All the houses have matching flowers. Sick, huh?"

"Definitely sick," Mike grunted. "Where's the key?"

"No key. No theft here, Mikey."

Mike opened the seafoam blue door, and they stepped in. Duke and Duchess ran to their dishes in an alcove. They wolfed down kibble.

The room was a sea of pastels. A peach sofa, one easy chair in pale yellow, another in pallid green, and the carpet, a washed-out blue. The walls were faded gold.

"I don't think much of the color scheme," Mike said. "Where's the kitchen?"

"No kitchen. Everyone eats out in Heaven. Nobody cooks."

Ruby walked down the hall. The bathroom was spacious: two sinks, a glassed-in shower, and a deep bathtub on clawed feet. "Nice," she said.

Buster trotted down the hall to the bedroom. "You're going to like this," he said.

Ruby looked in. "Oh-oh." Nauseous pinky-coral carpet and walls, frilly curtains, and flouncy bedspread in bilious variations of pink and coral gave her stomach an uneasy wrench.

"Mike, don't look. I can hardly stand it, and I have a cast-iron stomach. It looks like the inside of an internal organ. Buster, we can't live in this house. It's hideous!"

"Huh. Must be why it's available," Buster mused. "Well, no more empty cottages in this village. We'll check the next one, but do either of you speak German?"

"Of course not, silly dog. Are you telling us the next village is totally German?"

"The entire world population comes here. Not just English speakers. How about Portuguese? Lithuanian? Igbo?"

Ruby stopped Buster. "We'll live here. We'll keep our eyes closed. We just need to work fast. Meanwhile, let's go to breakfast. I'm hungry, in spite of . . . *that*."

Duke and Duchess crashed out on the peach sofa.

"Dad, we're tired. Can we stay here? You can whistle when you need us to come."

"I'm still amazed they talk to me. I'm not sure I like it."

"It's Heaven," Ruby said.

"Okay, troops," Buster said. "Onward to breakfast. I still don't understand why you didn't like that bedroom."

"For the same reason you like dog food, and we like people food," Ruby said.

"I like people food. It's you who doesn't like dog food."

"Well, that bedroom is dog food."

Another path led up the hill. At the top, they saw a larger ramada. It buzzed with people. The line reached all the way around the roofed area.

"Is there another one, Buster? It'll be hours before they can seat us."

"The next village will be the same. It's the breakfast hour."

Mike surprised her by saying he wanted to get in line. "I want to talk to people. We've only talked to Alice and Buster. Let's go."

They found the end of the line. Mike nodded to the guy they stepped behind. He was dressed in the same wheat color Mike wore.

"Scuse me," Mike said. "I'm Mike. This is Ruby. We just got here today. Does the line move fast?"

The young man turned and smiled. "Hi, folks. I'm Peter. No, it'll be a while before we see any grub." He ran his hand through brown, curly hair. Mike was tall, but Peter was basketball-player tall.

"Shoot," Mike said. "Wish I'd brought a sandwich with me before I . . . uh, cashed it in."

Peter hooted. "Yeah! Next time plan ahead, huh? You both cashed it in at the same time? That doesn't happen very often. You're lucky. That is . . . "

"Yep. We were lucky, huh, Ruby?" He turned and took her hand. She smiled.

"So Peter, do you like Heaven?" Mike asked.

"Oh, man! I love it here. No stress, no bills, everything's free. What's not to love?"

"And for fun?"

"Well . . . Skeeter and I hang out. We skateboard, flirt with chicks . . . er, girls. It's fun just being alive, man."

"Tell me, Peter, where can we find the art galleries?"

A frown creased Peter's brow. "Art galleries? I never saw one. What do you want with an art gallery?"

"I want a painting for my wall. Don't you have art on your walls?"

Peter scratched his head. He spoke to his friend. "Hey, Skeeter, do you have any art on your walls?"

"What?"

"Art. You know. Like a painting of a barn or a lighthouse."

"I know what art is, but I don't have any. Do you?"

Peter's frown deepened, as his unfocused eyes roved.

"What's the matter, Peter?" Mike asked. "You look . . . upset."

The man's eyes landed on Mike. "I . . . "

Mike waited. Peter's placid expression was gone.

"What have you done to him, Mike?" Ruby whispered.

"I'm not sure. I asked where the art galleries were. I must have struck a nerve."

"Or maybe a submerged memory."

# Chapter 18

"Hey, Skeeter, hold my place in line, will you? I need to see JD."
Peter grabbed his bicycle out of the rack and raced off.

Mike stepped into the gap. "Say, Skeeter," he said. "We just
got here today. Who's JD?"

Skeeter turned around. He reminded Mike of Jughead in the
Archie comic books. His beanie with zig-zag points completed
the image.

"He's the Head of Procurement. When anyone has a
suggestion, we go to him and he gets it for us. We get anything
we ask for. Cool, huh?" He gave Mike a lop-sided grin.

Mike turned around wondering if Heaven somehow let its
inhabitants slip back into their adolescence. Skeeter didn't come
across like any twenty-eight-year-old guy he knew in the real
world.

The line began to move. They rounded a corner and
advanced a few yards to a new side of the ramada. A group of
women joined the line.

Ruby turned and smiled at the woman behind her. "Hi," she
said to the pretty blond. "We just got here this morning. My
name's Ruby. Think there'll be any food left by the time we get
there?"

"Oh, it never runs out. As soon as the last breakfast person
gets served, lunch comes out. Non-stop food. My name's
Philly." Her hair cascaded from a yellow band.

"Like the horse?" Ruby asked.

Philly hooted. "No. I came here with no memory. They knew I lived in Philadelphia."

"Does it worry you?"

"Nobody worries here. All your phobias, insecurities, and issues fade into nothing. You're new but soon, you'll be just like us."

"Sounds . . . wonderful," Ruby lied. "I'm wondering, Philly." She whispered. "Does anyone fall in love?"

"Oh, sure! All the time. Look around. There are so many men and women here, the pickings are great. See that hunky George Clooney look-alike? I'm going to flirt with him today. Yum!"

"But I don't see any couples other than Mike and myself, and we got here together."

"Yeah. Well, we fall in love for a day and then it's over. I've fallen in love more times than I can count."

"Then don't you think it's just lust?"

Philly's face broke into a happy smile. "Nothing wrong with lust, huh? Lots more fun than love. Don't you agree?"

"Absolutely. But does anyone get pregnant?"

Philly's brows arched. "I've never heard of anyone getting preggers. Funny, huh? I guess it's not on the menu."

"A carefree life," Ruby commented. "No worries, no broken hearts, no deep, caring commitments, and no rosy-cheeked three-year-old to climb into your lap and call you Mommy."

Philly's eyes scanned the breakfast diners, but Ruby noticed the avidity fade from her face.

"Did you have children . . . before here?" Philly asked.

"No, but babies are definitely on my to-do list."

"Not while you're in Heaven," Philly murmured.

"No, but I don't plan to stay long."

Philly's hazel eyes scanned Ruby's blue ones. "You'd *leave* Heaven? I wouldn't know how. You sure you can?"

"I'll research it and get back to you. I've only been here since this morning. Ask me again in a week or a month if I still want to leave Heaven. I'm thinking how it would be to eat chocolate ice cream, exclusively. I'd love it at first, but at some point, I'd want a pastrami sandwich on rye with mustard and dill pickles.

"I love chocolate ice cream," the woman said. Especially if I'm licking it off George Clooney's uh . . . belly. Can't do *that* with a pastrami sandwich."

Another table of people left. The line advanced and turned another corner. Philly watched, as George left with his arm around a curvy redhead.

"Easy come, easy go, huh Philly?"

"Sure. Pretty boys are a dime a dozen."

"Why are we talking in clichés?"

They laughed. "You started it, Ruby." She looked down at the brick path. "I wish you weren't going. You're easy to talk to." She dropped her voice. "My friends and I, mostly giggle and flirt with every guy in sight. It gets old."

Peter rode up, parked his bike, and stepped between Skeeter and Mike. "Well, JD said there'd be no problem to get it okayed." He jammed his hands in his pockets with a big smile on his face.

"It's that easy to get anything you want?" Mike asked.

"Yeah. I can't believe I forgot. I was a successful artist. I want to get back into it. I asked for art supplies. Canvas, stretchers, oils, turp, an easel, and brushes. Why would JD turn me down? They're here to make us happy."

Finally, the next seven people, including Mike and Ruby, reached for trays and walked the food line, cafeteria style. The choices were everything anybody would want for breakfast, all hot and smelling delicious. Mike scooped perfect Eggs Benedict onto his plate, a biscuit, hashbrowns, and crisp bacon.

"Breakfast *and* lunch," he told Ruby. "I wonder where the food servers are."

An empty pan quietly sank under the counter, and a full pan of scrambled eggs rose.

"It seems that everything is engineered so there are no workers in Heaven."

"Maybe," Mike said. "After breakfast, we need to talk to JD."

"Who's JD?" Ruby spooned poached eggs onto multi-grain toast and lifted a glass of grapefruit juice onto her tray. They found an empty bench. Boisterous conversations swirled around them.

"Something to do with procurement. Let's talk later. I have an idea."

# Chapter 19

"How do we find this JD?" Ruby wondered aloud. "You could ask Peter."

"No, I don't want him to know we're going to see JD. Let's call Buster."

"Mike, you're suddenly helping me with the assignment. What changed?"

"I can't see the head honcho until I get indoctrinated. Your buddy, Abdul, told us not to get indoctrinated. Therefore, I'm stuck here. I'll pitch in so we can get back home a.s.a.p."

They took their trays and empty dishes to the "Trays Here" receptacle. The trays sank, and the cover slid closed.

"I want one of these when we get back home, Mike. It makes our dishwasher positively archaic."

"I'll ask JD to ship us one," Mike said, dryly. On the path, Mike whistled. Buster ran up with his tongue hanging out.

"Where were you?" Ruby asked.

"I've been cavorting with the cutest little apricot shit-poo."

"Buster, are you sure she didn't say she's a shih tzu? It doesn't matter. We need to get an appointment with JD."

"No need. I'll take you to his house. Come on."

Buster trotted down the path, and after twenty rows of houses, they turned and followed past seventeen pastel-hued cottages to a pale yellow one, surrounded by yellow hollyhocks.

"Buster, how did you find this house? There are no numbers, names, or identifying markers."

"Easy. Put the person's name in your mind, and you'll be led to the right house."

"So if I wanted to go to Peter's house and there was more than one Peter, what then?"

"Just put his image in your mind. Now, I've got a date with a little honey, who thinks I'm the hottest thing since Cholula sauce." He pranced away.

"Mike, we need to talk about your idea before we face him."

"Don't worry, Ruby. Just go along with me. If it works, it will be a baby step."

Ruby looked worried, but she knocked on the yellow door. When it opened, she did a double take, sure she would have heard if Johnny Dep had bitten the big one. And yet . . . those eyes.

"You're . . . "

"JD. Who were you expecting?"

"What does JD stand for?"

"John Doe. Does that tell you about my demise? They never knew who I was. JD sounds better, don't you think? Come in. What can I do for you?"

The room was an exact duplicate of the living room in their cottage. "Same decorator," Ruby murmured.

"JD, Peter just came to you and asked for art supplies, right?" Mike asked.

"Yes. Excellent suggestion. Heaven should have an art supply station in every village. I'm sure there are lots of artists who'll be pleased."

"Yes," Mike answered. "JD, are you aware that hardly any souls are leaving Heaven? It's becoming overly crowded at an alarming rate. It took us what felt like an hour to get breakfast."

"And I'm responsible for that?"

"Not at all. Am I correct that the only way to leave Heaven is to be reborn?"

"It's the only way I know of," JD responded.

"And your position as a procurer is to supply everything anyone wants, except for a loving marriage and babies, of course, so they'll be lulled into staying in Heaven?"

"Well, yes. Is that bad?"

"No," Mike answered. "Except that life here is *too* good. Nobody needs to strive for anything. People can regress to when Mommy and Daddy handed everything to them on a silver platter, and they didn't need to overcome problems. Actually, easier than many children had it."

"I don't remember even *having* a childhood," JD said softly.

"Do you ever think that if you went back you'd have a better life?" Mike asked.

"I'd have to think about that," he mused. "So, what do you suggest I do?"

"Peter wants to get back to his art. That was the best part of his life. Don't give him art supplies. Tell him to get reborn, and he'll be a better, more successful artist in his next life if he works at it. He might even be a child prodigy."

JD stared at Mike. "Do you think that's how Michelangelo became a master? Van Gogh? Warhol? But Mike, maybe they perfected their creativity and skills in Heaven."

"It's possible," Ruby admitted.

"My job isn't to solve the population explosion. I'm the village procurer. I'll call a council of the procurers in all the other villages, and we'll kick around your idea. But I'm certain they'll think as I do."

"We took the last house available in this village. What if there's a world pandemic? Where would thousands of new souls live?"

"I don't know. Not my department. Now, excuse me. I need to call a meeting."

"How do you call a meeting, JD, with no phones? Mental telepathy?"

"Come with me. I'll show you something about Heaven."

They trekked out onto the lawn. JD crouched, then sprang into the air and floated away. He waved to Mike and Ruby's astonished faces and slowly vanished. His grinning mouth was the last thing to fade away.

"Well," Ruby said when she could speak again. "I know where Lewis Carroll got his Cheshire cat idea. Think we can do that?"

"Ruby," Mike said, "Think of this. Heaven is about to become standing room only."

# Chapter 20

"Come on, Ruby. Let's see if we can find our cottage. We need to regroup."

"Uh . . . according to Buster, we can just imagine who we want to see, and our minds will lead us there. You think of me, and I'll think of you."

"Got it. Let's go."

He headed east, and Ruby turned west and took a few steps. They turned and looked at each other and grinned.

"I guess there are two ways to get there."

"I'll go your way."

When they arrived at their cottage, Duke and Duchess were lying on the grass under a tree. Their long red tongues were hanging out. "We're tired, and hungry, Dad. Where were you? We want in."

"Mike, before we go in . . . "

"What, Ruby?"

"Uh, do you think we can fly like JD?"

He looked into her eyes. "Do you want to fly?"

"Let's try it."

"Okay. But let's hold hands. I don't want to fly away without you."

Ruby felt a rush of . . . love?

"Right. I don't want to fly off without you, either."

They took each other's hand. "Okay, JD crouched before he pushed off. When I say one, we'll crouch, and when I say three, push off. Ready?"

"Ready."

"One . . . two . . . three!"

They pushed off, left the sidewalk, and hovered a foot above for five seconds before gently descending.

The dogs danced around their feet, barking.

"Wow! That was wild! We got off the ground, Mike. Woo-hoo!"

"Maybe it takes practice. Let's try again later. I'm dying of thirst. I hope this cottage has a water faucet."

They found a water dispenser and glasses. Both chugged the first drink and took a second one to the sofa. The dogs gobbled their kibble and drank from the perpetually full water bowl. They flopped down and instantly fell asleep.

"What are we going to do, Ruby? My big idea went down the tubes. Now the arts will flourish and everyone will be more contented than before."

"It was worth a try, Mike. We need to sow discontent somehow. What's missing in Heaven that they can only have on Earth? I wish I had some popcorn. I think better if I'm snacking on something warm and buttery. Maybe that's what's missing."

"Good idea, but if we point it out, someone will go to JD, and he'll put popcorn dispensers on every corner."

"Oh, right." They were quiet. "Even if we could come up with the thing that JD couldn't supply and that everyone would want, how could we sell it?"

"Sell it?" Mike asked.

"Present it so everyone would see what important thing's missing in their lives that Heaven can't supply."

"First things first, Ruby. We need to figure out what *it* is. Then we'll work on how to sell it. Right?"

"Right . . . but I'm foggy. I feel a nap coming on." She snuggled into Mike.

"Let's do this right," he said. "I'll carry you over the threshold of the bedroom."

She smiled and put her arms around his neck. "I think you're supposed to do that after the . . . " she murmured into his chest.

"We'll pretend," he whispered. He carried her to the bed. "Do you want to nap or . . . ?

"Or. Definitely or." They did nap, later. When she opened her eyes, Mike was awake, leaning on one elbow, looking at her.

"What?" she said.

"I was thinking."

"Don't be enigmatic. Thinking about what?"

"What you said earlier, about finding what they can get, only after being reborn. It needs to be important. They can get all the frivolous things they want, right here."

"Here's what I think, Mike. We need more research. Talk to more people. So far, we've only scratched the surface. I wonder where people gather other than in the food ramada."

"Buster will know. Let's go. But I don't want to walk. Too slow. I've seen bicycles, skates, skateboards, and trikes. Name your poison."

"I haven't been on any of those since I was a kid. We might as well get pogo sticks. Can you get skinned knees in Heaven?"

"I'll requisition a bicycle with a sidecar from JD."

"With an umbrella. And a minibar. I'll mix drinks while you pedal."

"We'll be very popular. Think we can get kicked out of Heaven?"

"Not yet, Mike. We have work to do."

# Chapter 21

After they showered and changed into clean clothes, Ruby looked at Mike. "I wonder if we'll remember Heaven when we go back to Denver."

"Why wouldn't we? It's not like we're going through conception, birth, and childhood again. If you're ready, let's go find Buster."

They stepped out, and Ruby put her hand on Mike's arm.

"You know, if we could fly we wouldn't need wheels. We said we'd try again."

"Okay." Mike took her hand. "One, two, three!" They jumped into the air, and . . . hovered.

"Are we stuck?" Ruby whispered.

"I don't know. Let's try something. Remember Superman always put one arm out the way he wanted to fly. Let's point up."

They each pointed an arm up. "This feels stupid!" Ruby said.

They didn't fly at the speed of Superman but drifted up. When they were higher than the rooftops, they pointed up the hill.

"I feel like I'm dreaming," Ruby called. "I love this! I want to keep going."

They drifted over the rows of houses and saw the food ramada. People were standing in line for lunch.

"What if they can see us, Mike?"

"JD faded away. Maybe we're invisible. We'll soon find out."

They drifted over the crowd. No one looked up. Mike and Ruby grinned at each other.

"Let's fly over the village, Mike. I wonder if there's a way to speed up. At this rate, it would take us hours."

"No gas pedal. Try with both arms out."

They dropped each other's hands and extended both arms in front. The acceleration was gradual but steady.

"How fast are we going to go?" Ruby called. They were gaining speed.

"I don't know. No manual," he shouted. "Try slowly lowering your arms!"

They matched their arm levels and decelerated to a comfortable speed.

"Which direction should we go?"

"I want to see the German village," Ruby said. "Let's keep going this way. I have a feeling it's just over the horizon."

They flew over cottages that stretched as far as they could see. They saw another food ramada with people in two lines and still no end of the pastel cottages.

"How long have we been up, Mike?"

He checked his watch. "Oh, right. It stopped when we woke in Heaven. How much longer do you want to keep going?"

"Let's speed up until we're over the next village."

They raised their arms slowly until they whizzed along. Mike kept glancing to see if Ruby was ready to slow down, but she had a look of pure joy on her face. Her blond hair streamed straight out behind.

"Ruby," Mike shouted, "Let's slow down."

"Why? There's no traffic, no dangerous road conditions, and no speed limits. Want to see how fast we can go?"

"Not really," he shouted. "What I *want* is to get back to our un-celestial lives. Besides, we don't know how many more miles there are of this village. It may take a week to get to the German village. We don't have that kind of time. Let's turn around and zoom back. "

Ruby gave him a sheepish grin. "You're right. I got carried away. Come on, I'll race you back."

They zoomed back, playfully cutting in front of each other, flying inches above each another, and nudging shoulders in mock battles. They almost missed their ramada.

"Look! There's Duke and Duchess. Let's go down."

"Do we know how? I don't want to *fall* to the ground."

"Ruby, we can't die in Heaven. Try lowering your arms."

It worked and they descended. Ruby's eyes were on the dogs, and she misjudged the closeness of the ground. She landed on her hands and knees. "Ouch! That hurt."

One knee of her pants was torn. The heels of her hands were red.

Duchess ran to her and licked her face. "Whacha doin' on the ground, Mom?"

"I fell out of the sky, Duch. What have you been doing?"

"We've been playing and playing. I love this place. We made friends with a boxer and a real goofy great dane."

"Don't get too used to it. This is just a vacation. Oh, look. There's Buster."

"Hi, Buster. Where's your girlfriend?"

"She gave me the slip. Said she didn't want to go steady."

"Are you broken-hearted?"

"Naw. I have my eye on a feisty Papillion. She has the cutest ears."

"Buster," Ruby said, "you look thinner. Go to the house to eat now and then."

"Oh, sure. Don't worry about me . . . Coco! Over here. It's loverboy!"

They watched Buster prance over to the brown and white dog with the high-flying ears.

"Speaking of eating, I'm hungry. Let's get in line for dinner."

They walked back to the ramada and joined the queue. "I miss being able to eat at home," Mike murmured.

"Me too, but this way there's plenty of time to talk to people."

She turned to the man who joined the line behind her.

He had thick, curly black hair and a massive mustache.

"Hi! My name's Ruby. You look like a musician I used to know. Is there a place where we can listen to live music? I feel like getting my dancing shoes on. You know, prance around like nobody's watching."

He frowned and turned to the man behind him. "Hey Jim, is there a place where we can listen to live music?"

He turned back to Ruby. "I'm Carlos. I'm . . . or I *was*, a guitarist, and a damned good one. I'd forgotten that. I wonder why?"

His friend joined the conversation. "I haven't heard of any." He gave Ruby an appraising look so intense, she felt slightly uncomfortable. "I'm Jimbo, and who are you, pretty lady?

"Hi Jimbo. I'm Ruby. This is my, uh, boyfriend, Mike. We just got here, and we're still trying to get the lay of the land."

The line moved up and Mike started talking to the woman ahead of him. When Ruby looked back, Jimbo had traded places with Carlos. He'd released his ponytail. Long, blond curls framed a distinctly feral face.

"Look, Babe," he whispered, "when you dump Mikey, come see me. I'm the only Jimbo in the village. Got it?"

"What makes you think I'm going to dump my boyfriend? I'm sure you're a lovely man, but don't hold your breath waiting for me."

Jimbo threw his long face back and laughed, showing horsey teeth.

"Just sayin'," he said. "See? He already picked up on the chick in front of him."

"Tell me something, Jimbo. Do you believe in love? The kind that lasts?"

He looked at her like she'd sprouted an extra head.

"Why limit myself to one woman? Does a bee just visit one flower?"

"Your logic is flawed, Jimbo. Bees that visit flowers are females, and they're not there for sex."

Ruby didn't wait for his comeback. She stepped up and attempted to join the conversation with Mike, but instead of a conversation, it was a lament. Mike shot Ruby a look that said, *get me out of this.*

"Hi, I'm Mike's girlfriend. Is Heaven living up to your expectations?"

"Expectations!" she sputtered. "Who knew what to expect? We're fed a bunch of crap about harp music, winged Angels and eternal bliss. This is supposed to be our reward for living? Some reward! We stand in line half of our time and the other half, we do absolutely nothing. It's so boring, if I could kill myself again, I would."

"You could always sign up to get reborn."

"I hated my life. I would rather . . . " she stopped, unable to name anything worse.

"You were so unhappy with life you ended it thinking Heaven would be your refuge but now . . . oh look. Lucky you. You're next for dinner."

She stomped away. Mike looked relieved. "I never thought about anybody not liking Heaven."

"Mike, after dinner let's find the Rebirth Center. I have an idea."

They were finally in. The dinner choices were sumptuous. Mike chose a T-bone steak, mashed potatoes, and two dinner rolls.

Ruby eyed his tray. "Where do you think the meat comes from . . . a slaughterhouse in Heaven?"

"Maybe it's plant-based meat. But we don't see any vegetable farms either. I guess there are some mysteries here we're not meant to know."

She chose broiled salmon and spinach. They both splurged on warm pecan pie with a slice of cheese.

"I'm stuffed."

"Me too. Let's walk to the Rebirth Center. I need the exercise."

They whistled for Buster and all three dogs came. "Buster, we want to find the Rebirth Center. Duke and Duchess, come with us."

"It's up the hill," Buster said. "I'll take you there."

They hoofed it up the path, the poodles prancing beside them. They were quiet so Alice wouldn't come out of the next cottage with her clipboard.

"Thanks, Buster. You all wait here for us," Ruby whispered.

The dogs sat down in the shade of a large Ficus tree and Mike knocked on the door. They waited. And waited. Finally, the door opened.

"Yes?" said the man who stuck his head out. He looked up at Mike with large brown eyes. "Oh! You want to be reborn? Sorry. Where are my manners? Come in, come in. My name's

Georgie." He extended his hand and shook Mike's and then Ruby's.

They followed him into his cottage. "Tea? Coffee? Gin and tonic? Sorry. I'm out of gin *and* tonic. I haven't had any for, oh . . . six years. I still miss it."

"Tea would be fine if it's no trouble. We're here on a special mission. Georgie, can you keep an important secret?"

"Not until I have a cup of tea." He turned on the tea kettle. They sat down at the round table as their host set out cups, a caddy of tea bags, and a sugar bowl. They chose their teas as the kettle whistled. Georgie poured and sat in the third chair. He was a small man. His tightly curled mop of brown hair hadn't seen scissors in a long time.

"You've been in Heaven for six years?"

"Maybe. No way to tell. How many years has it been for you?"

"Georgie, I'm going to tell you our secret. We just arrived today. We've been chosen to come here to solve the overcrowding problem. You can help, immensely."

"Me?" His caterpillar brows shot up.

"How many people have you helped get reborn this week?"

"Um . . . a grand total of . . . let's see . . . uh, none."

"So Georgie," Ruby said, "the problem is, that like you, everybody gets to Heaven and stays, year after year. Have you ever considered going back for another life? You know, gin and tonics, a tall stature, another shot at love and a family?"

A nostalgic look crossed his face. "I could, couldn't I?"

"Here's an idea. When people come to Heaven, do you think there should be a set time they can stay?"

His round eyes got large. "Like how long?"

"We don't know. A year? Eighteen months?" Mike shook his head.

"That would work for the newbies, but what about everyone who's already here? What do we do with them? We can't *make* them volunteer."

"That's it. We haven't come up with the answer to that one. Any suggestions?"

But Georgie's mind was elsewhere. He grinned at them, and danced a little jig, snapping his fingers at either side of his head.

"Tell you what, folks. I've turned the Rebirth Center over to you. Good luck!"

He turned a cartwheel and skipped down the hall. One second later, they heard a sonorous gong.

Mike and Ruby found Georgie's clothes lying in the center of a twinkling circle on the floor.

# Chapter 22

"Mike, we can't be stuck in the Rebirth Center. What in Heaven's name are we going to do?"

"We should go see Alice in Indoctrination and tell her Georgie abandoned his post in favor of rebirth. We don't need to tell her he appointed us as the new directors."

"What if she insists we get indoctrinated?"

"We'll tell her we're under strict orders to stay un-indoctrinated."

They stepped out into the unrelenting blue sky. The dogs were waiting in the shade. "Buster, take Duke and Duchess to our cottage. You all need to eat and rest. Did you drink any water today?"

"Sure, Mom. There are water dishes everywhere," Duke assured her, "but I'm hungry and I need a nap."

"Come on, I'll show you a shortcut," Buster said. They loped off, tongues hanging out.

"Oh, you're finally here," Alice said when she opened the door of her cottage.

Her formerly apple-green hair, now hot pink, was arranged on top of her head in loops and swirls.

"Alice, do you know Abdul?" Ruby asked.

She stared at Ruby with big eyes. "How do *you* know Abdul?"

"It's a long story. The important thing is that he *sent* us here to solve the overcrowding problem. He told us not to get indoctrinated. We didn't get here the usual way."

"Please come in and have a seat," she said. "I'll fix us tea and we can talk." Her elaborate hairstyle sported Cupie curls which bounced as she walked.

The room was a warm terra-cotta color. The white sofa was strewn with pillows. Ruby and Mike shed their shoes and left them on the doorstep. Their feet sank into the pristine white carpeting.

"This room is beautiful," Ruby said, admiring the abstract art in strong slashes of deep colors, hanging on the wall. "Who's the artist?"

"I dabble when I have time," Alice called from the kitchen. She came in carrying a tray with a teapot. To Ruby, Alice didn't look twenty-eight. She had faint crow's feet and the tendons in her hands were pronounced.

"I would say you're more than a dabbler. Your art is beautiful."

"Let's talk about your mission." Her green eyes looked from Mike to Ruby. "Have you come to any conclusions?"

"We're still learning about Heaven, Alice. We went to the Rebirth Center to talk to Georgie, but he walked off and disappeared into thin air while we were there. Does he do that or was this . . ."

"Quite unexpected! I've never heard him talk about rebirthing himself. What did you talk about?"

"About setting a time limit for new entrants to stay in Heaven. Do you think it's a good idea? It could be part of the indoctrination."

Before Alice answered Mike's question, Ruby spoke.

"What happened to Georgie's body? All we found were his clothes."

"Ruby, although the people here look like their twenty-eight-year-old former selves, they're actually the souls they take from life to life. Their *essence*. So when Georgie rebirthed, what looked like his body, went back into . . . sort of a bank. His essence has chosen what will be a newborn to go back into the physical world."

"Wow," Ruby whispered.

"Next question," Alice prompted.

"We noticed that the people we've talked to seem to be obsessed with quickie hook-ups and then they flit off. Why is that? It seems rather shallow."

"You noticed that? Did you also notice that Heaven doesn't have alcohol, opioids, tobacco, prescription drugs, marijuana, psilocybin mushrooms, heroin, I could go on and on, but I think you get it. What Heaven *does* have is sex. Consensual sex, no pregnancies, no STDs, and no societal shame."

"So it's a trade-off. I guess I get it."

"Now, my question. How do you know Abdul?"

Ruby told Alice about her metaphysical prize and Abdul's mentoring, disguised as a Moroccan cab driver. "I told him I would consider occasional projects when I resigned, and here we are. Mike didn't want me to go, so as a compromise, he came too. Buster came as our guide, and our dogs, Duke and Duchess are here. They love Heaven."

"I presume Abdul thought as outsiders, your evaluation might shine a clearer light on a solution. Why didn't he come?"

Ruby noticed a tiny snide inflection.

"Alice, we're here to look and learn. You know everything about Heaven and we know nothing, so let's collaborate. Together, we can surely come up with a great answer."

Mike set his cup down. "I have questions. We arrived this morning. This has been the longest day I've ever had. I'm exhausted. When does it get dark here?"

"It doesn't, Mike. You've been here three days. When people come to Heaven the usual way, they don't think of day and night. They eat when they're hungry and sleep when they're tired. They aren't governed by sundown or sunrise. Have you noticed there are no shadows? No sun, no dark, no moon, no stars. Robin-egg blue sky constantly. Also, there's no weather. No wind, rain, snow, excessive heat or cold."

They sat quietly and looked at each other.

"Alice, I have the feeling you've been here longer than anyone. What's the deal? Have you ever considered rebirthing?"

She looked at Mike, pushed a strand of pink hair back from her face and took a sip of her tea.

"You've heard of St. Peter? There's no such person and no pearly gate. I'm the welcoming committee. No soul gets turned away from Heaven. What I do is," she paused, "you've heard that people's lives flash before their eyes when they're dying?"

Ruby and Mike nodded, wide-eyed.

"That's not true. It happens when they get here. I show them their lives. If there are parts that hurt people, it slows down and they see in vivid detail the pain and harm they caused."

"But they don't get turned away?" Ruby asked. "They don't go to . . . Hell?"

"Hell would mean their souls would never get a chance to learn from their mistakes. Heaven is a chance to do better next time. Makes better sense, doesn't it?"

"So Alice," Ruby asked, "How long did it take for Hitler to see all his mistakes?"

"He died April thirtieth, 1945. He's still in review mode."

112

"I guess that means his soul won't be eligible to be released into the world for a long time."

"A long, l-o-n-g time. He needs to apologize to all those souls. And he must *really* mean it. Redemption for Adolph may *not* happen."

"What's Life Review like, Alice? Is it . . . a little like Hell?"

"It's not *called* Hell, Ruby, but it's not exactly fun, either."

"So." Mike picked up the conversation after a quiet pause while he and Ruby thought about this revelation. "Eighteen months after Life Review unless, of course, there's a desire to go back earlier. Does that sound about right?"

"We can try it, Mike. If it doesn't work, we'll adjust. The *real* problem is how do we motivate the ones already here? What can we promise to give them that's better than Heaven?"

"Well," Ruby said, "there's fine wine or in Georgie's case, gin and tonics. There's recreational marijuana, fast cars, starry skies, the moon . . . and real love."

"Yes, but there's also mortgages, hurricanes, boring jobs, bad marriages, high blood pressure, varicose veins . . . shall I go on?"

"But Alice, challenges are what make us resourceful. Humans need the rewards of overcoming adversity. They don't get that here. It's too easy, too vanilla. Where are the exciting scientific discoveries, wonderful literature, breathtaking sculptures, poetry, art, and beautiful music? Another thing. Do you remember how good it feels to get home after a vacation?"

Alice frowned. Mike and Ruby waited.

"Okay," she finally spoke, her voice husky. "How do we convince them?"

113

# Chapter 23

After another interesting conversation in the line queuing for lunch, Mike and Ruby finally sat at a table. Mike was quiet, eating slowly, not particularly interested in his food.

"I think I've got it, Rube. He told her his idea, and then, they were both excited.

"We should tell Alice, Mike. It might be the answer to return Heaven to a temporary respite instead of a permanent home."

"And our ticket back to Denver."

They walked to Alice's cottage and knocked on the door. Her hair, now dazzling blond, was in dozens of thin braids tied together on top of her head.

"We think we have it, Alice."

"Come in! Tell me everything."

She offered them coffee or tea. They declined. She sank to a hassock and waited.

"Tell her, Mike. It was your plan."

"Alice, everyone we've talked to in the food line has forgotten about their former lives. Is this deliberate?"

"Dying can be traumatic, Mike. We want their entrance to be peaceful."

"But the amnesia seems to hang on. I want to jog people's memories. Remind them of what they left behind so they'll want to go back and build on their successes . . . *or* choose another path if their life wasn't fulfilling. Doing it one person at a time in the food line is too slow. What if we set up on a popular path and interview people? Others might gather around and listen.

"There's television here, right Alice? Could we film the interviews and show them on TV? Others might remember *their* lives. Does everyone know they can reincarnate and how it's done?"

Alice steepled her fingers. "I'm not sure a TV show's the Heavenly way."

"Alice, the Heavenly way is too burdensome. Before Georgie went home, he told us no one had rebirthed the entire week. How many have rebirthed after he left?"

"Hmm, I see your point but my fear is . . . uh," her voice trailed off.

"Let's try it as an experiment, Alice," Ruby proposed. "We could interview say, ten people. Out of those interviews, we choose five to air on a new TV show we'll call *Your Life* or something clever. I think it should be a regular show. We could do it for a while, see if there are any results, adverse or beneficial, and go from there."

"What about the other villages who don't speak English?" Alice asked.

"How do they watch the other TV shows? Isn't there dubbing or subtitles?"

"Hmm. You're right." She frowned. "I'll present the idea to the Board of Directors. They might vote no."

Mike and Ruby looked at each other. *Board of Directors?*

"Tell us about this board, Alice," Ruby asked. "Who are they? How often do they meet?" She was imagining patriarchs with long white beards.

"Each village has its own board, volunteers of four women and four men. Everybody can attend, take part in discussions, present a desired action, argue for or against a pending motion, or just listen and enjoy the refreshments."

"How often do things get done?" Mike asked.

Alice looked out the window and said, "Now and then."

"When was the last motion?" Ruby probed.

Alice looked away. "Um, quite some time ago. They voted to plant pansies along the walks instead of four o'clocks."

"Good decision. When's the next meeting?"

"I'm . . . not . . . sure. The last one was canceled. It was a no-show.

"So basically, there's not much interest in changing Heaven. Right?"

"You might say that."

"Okay," Mike said. "Thanks. Notify us if the board calls a meeting."

Ruby and Mike said goodbye and left. "What are we going to do, Mike?"

"There's one way to see if the board will stop us. Buster can take us to the TV studio. Once we get that person on board, I'll write my interview and practice it until it sounds unscripted. You can be the camera person. Okay?"

"With one of those big cameras that sits on the shoulder? I'd need to get prepped on the operation and then spend some time practicing . . . this is exciting!"

They walked down the slope, noticing pansies blooming by the path. Not a four o'clock in sight.

Buster suddenly appeared, trotting across the grass. "Here I am," he said.

"How'd you do that, Buster?" Mike asked. "I was about to whistle for you."

"Follow me. I'll take you there."

"Take us where?"

"To the television station, of course."

"Thank you, Buster. Did you listen to us in Alice's house?"

Buster didn't reply but kept up his fast-paced trot down a path. He delivered them to a cottage with a large sign proclaiming to be KHEV-TV. He stopped and sat beside the door.

"I'm just doing my job . . . rather well. Right? He's waiting for you. Go on in." Buster turned and trotted away.

"I think . . . he's reporting back to Abdul or . . . he can't *be* Abdul, can he? They have the same brown eyes . . . ."

The cottage was painted a brash mustard color. They stepped in.

"WELCOME TO KHEV!" the man at the desk shouted. "I'M FRANKIE AND YOU'RE MIKE AND RUBY." His straw-yellow hair stuck out in all directions like he'd spent all day at the beach. His ruddy complexion and washed-out blue eyes gave him the look of a lifeguard.

"Nice to meet you, Frankie. How do you know our names?"

"YOUR GUIDE, OF COURSE. NOW, LET'S SIT DOWN AND TALK."

Mike and Ruby looked at each other with raised eyebrows and followed Frankie to a mustard-colored sofa.

"Frankie," Mike started, "Ruby and I have only been here a few days and we haven't had time to watch much TV. What kinds of shows do you run?"

"Mostly old classics. Lawrence Welk, Petticoat Junction and," he paused, eyes sparkling, "My favorite . . . Gilligan's Isle!"

"We'd like to propose a new show to you. It would be—"

Frankie interrupted, "AN INTERACTIVE SHOW OF AMBUSH INTERVIEWS WITH THE RESIDENTS. RIGHT?" Frankie shouted. "IT WON'T WORK!"

Frankie, do you know what everybody in Heaven is thinking?" Ruby asked.

"OF COURSE NOT."

"Then why do you say it won't work? Wouldn't you be interested in hearing what some of the residents did in their former lives? What did *you* do, before coming to Heaven? Something really interesting, I bet." She smiled at him.

He stopped, opened his mouth, closed it, and stared into Ruby's eyes. His face turned red.

"Let's give it a few shows to see if it gets viewers," Ruby continued. "Mike was a TV personality in Denver. He can be the interviewer. I'll be the camera person. I'll need operating instructions and some time to—"

Frankie interrupted, "I'M SORRY, MY DEAR BUT IT TAKES YEARS OF INTENSIVE TRAINING TO BE A PROFESSIONAL CAMERA PERSON. AS I SAID, IT WON'T WORK."

"How is your viewership, Frankie?" Mike asked. "Could you stand having a venue that would get people excited to watch a new show that talks to their friends and neighbors about their lives?"

"And you're absolutely right, Frankie," Ruby added. "We don't have time to train me to do everything to make a production look professional. I'd hate to turn it into a comedy. You're the expert. *You* be the cameraman."

# Chapter 24

Mike and Ruby left the TV studio. Frankie said he would need some time to think over their proposal.

"That didn't go very well," Ruby said. "I feel like someone got to Frankie before we got there and twisted his arm."

"To thwart our plan?"

"I don't know . . . he already knew our names. That was strange. And when you asked him how he knew the details about our proposal, he said our guide told him. Does that make sense to you, Mike? I'm going to talk to Buster. Something's not adding up."

Mike whistled his special Buster whistle. They walked on, but Buster didn't show.

"I'm not hungry, but let's get in the dinner line. We'll talk to Buster when he comes to the cottage tonight."

They joined the line at the food ramada. "I'll practice my interview technique," Mike whispered.

"Hi," he said to the man in front of him. "My name's Mike. I just arrived a few days ago. This place is a trip! I think we got the last available cottage. Did you wait long for one when you got here?"

The man turned around, looked at Mike, and then saw Ruby standing quietly behind him.

With eyes glued to her, he said, "Uh, no. I actually had choices." He was short and had a barrel chest. He'd cut his pale green tunic into a tank top. His hirsute back and shoulders needed mowing.

Mike plowed on, although he saw the guy was distracted. "That's cool," he said. "I guess the place is filling up. How long have you been here?"

"Want to go ahead of me?" the hairy guy asked.

Ruby, seeing what was happening, wandered away and sat on a bench out of sight.

"Okay," Mike stepped in front of him. "How long did you say you've been here?"

"Shoot," the hapless man said and then looked at Mike. "What did you say?"

"I asked how long you've been in Heaven."

The man frowned and scratched his head, leaving his brown hair in a stand-up swirl. "You know, I never thought of it, but I don't know if it's been two months or ten years. Why do you ask?"

"I don't know how long I want to stay before I get reborn and have another life," Mike said. "What did you do in your life journey?"

The man, who hadn't told Mike his name, looked at his feet. He'd cut his shoes into crude sandals.

"In one life," his eyes were unfocused and he spoke quietly, "I was a stone mason like my father. We helped build massive cathedrals . . . in Italy."

"A noble profession," Mike said. "And then?" he prompted.

"I remember cutting stones for streets."

"A different life? Where were you?"

"Yeah. Still in Italy. Not such a good life."

"What did you do in your last life?" Mike softly asked.

He closed his eyes, remembering. "I was an engineer. I designed tunnels. And dams. Huge concrete dams."

"Do you miss it?"

The man opened his eyes and looked at Mike. "Hell yes, I miss it!"

"Look," Mike said. "Would you be interested in being interviewed for a TV show I'm starting? I would ask you the questions we were just talking about. I think your life experiences would be interesting for everyone to hear about."

"Sorry, I don't think I'll be here." He walked off.

Mike watched him breeze past Ruby without a glance.

"Where is he going?" She asked, joining him back in the line.

He grinned. "He remembered some long ago lives and then I asked about his last life. He was a structural engineer. I asked if he missed it. I think he's going up to get reborn."

"Mike, nobody's in the Rebirth Center. We better tell Alice."

"Call Buster. He can run faster. Damn! I wish we had our phones."

"On my way!" Buster called out as he ran by at top speed.

Mike and Ruby looked at each other.

"I'm not complaining," Ruby said, "but do you get the feeling that Buster is ... I don't know."

They'd reached the food so they each picked up a tray, a plate, and utensils. Mike chose French fries. Ruby helped herself to a green salad.

"Shall we eat here or fly back to the cottage?"

"Let's eat here. I might get another chance to practice."

"Okay. Hope I don't need to get lost again."

Mike gave her a wink. "Just look bitchy if my interviewee starts ogling you."

"Okay. I'll start with whiney. Then I'll advance to bitchy."

"Fine. But don't shut down the interview."

They found two spaces in the middle of a crowded table. Mike sat down by a woman.

"My first interview of a woman," he murmured.

"Everything smells really good." Ruby said. "I didn't think I was hungry. The food here tastes better than the food in Denver. Why do you think?"

"I don't know. No bathroom scales." He paused. "Watch this." He turned to the woman beside him.

"Hi," he said to the attractive woman. "I'm Mike."

"Hi yourself, Mike," she had a deep voice and long, dark lashes over periwinkle blue eyes. Auburn hair set off her dusky complexion.

Mike cleared his throat. "I've only been here a few days. I'm still getting . . . acclimated. How long have you been—"

She interrupted, "My name's Cheri." She pronounced it, Cher-ee.

"Th-thanks, Cheri'. How long have you been—"

Cheri reached over and took one of his French fries, bit it in half and slowly put the rest in his mouth. She smiled.

"Mikeee," Ruby whined. "Can you get me some lemon slices?"

He turned to her. "When you get them, get me some more French fries."

"Oh! So *that's* how it is. You'd rather talk to *her* than me!"

"Okay, Ruby," he said under his breath. "She knows I'm with you now, okay?"

But Cheri had turned away, talking to the woman beside her.

"Let's eat and go back to the cottage, Mike. You'll do better with women when you have a microphone and a cameraman. I can't blame miss horny-toad. You're devastatingly handsome."

"I guess she thought I was coming on to her." He ate a French fry. "Do you really need more lemon?"

"No Mikee," she said in a whiny voice. "I didn't want you to share any more spit with Cher-eee."

Mike grinned.

Holding hands on the path back to their cottage, they were quiet. Pansies bloomed alongside the mown grass, stretching to the horizon. Mike wondered why they never saw the yard crew.

"I had one hit and one miss, but I learned what to do and what not to do. The day has been a success, I'd say."

"I agree," Ruby said. "I wonder if the engineer managed to get reborn."

"We'll ask Buster. He seems to know everything before we do."

"I've been thinking about that, Mike. I'm getting the feeling that Abdul has something to do with . . . "

"Abdul? But he said he couldn't come here, remember? Something about politics."

"Right, but I have a theory. I'm tired and sleepy. Is it the end of the day yet? I miss sundown and night. I want to go home. Colorado home."

"I feel the same way." He put his arm around her shoulder and they walked to the cottage in companionable silence.

"Dogs! We're home! Anybody want to go out and get some fresh air?"

The poodles were happy to see their humans. Buster, asleep on the sofa, didn't stir.

"I'll take them out," Mike said. "You go to bed."

"Thanks. I want to talk to Buster." She sat beside him on the sofa.

"Abdul," she said in his ear, "We may need your help with Frankie."

125

# Chapter 25

Buster raised his head, looked at Ruby, and winked. He put his head down and closed his eyes.

"I *knew* it! You can't come here as yourself so you've come as Buster. Wait until I tell Mike."

Buster growled.

"I can't tell Mike? Is that what you mean? Talk to me, Abdul."

Mike, Duke, and Duchess burst into the cottage. The dogs were panting, and Mike was breathing hard. "We were playing tag," he said. "They always got me. I'm beat!"

"Mike, wait 'til . . . "

Buster barked, louder than Ruby had ever heard him. In fact, she realized, she'd never heard him bark.

"Okay, Buster! You can stop now," she yelled.

He stopped, curled up, and went back to sleep.

"What were you about to tell me?" Mike asked.

"I was going to say we should go to the TV station tomorrow, and tell Frankie we're going to start the interviews. You can cite your success with the engineer."

"Huh. Let's sleep on it Ruby, and decide in the morning, uh . . . when we wake up. I'm ready to get this show on the road. But, right now, I need a shower and a pillow."

They showered together, soaped each other, giggling like kids, and then slid into bed. Ruby snuggled next to Mike.

"You know what else Heaven doesn't have?" Ruby asked when they woke.

"Mice?"

"Well, that too, but what I'm missing are smells."

"You miss smells? Like what?"

"You're going to laugh, but I miss your pits in the morning."

"I can't believe you said that." Mike sniffed at his armpits. "I don't smell anything."

"That's my point."

Mike laughed. "You're right. One more reason to wrap this up and get the hell out of here . . . maybe we miss these things because we didn't get to Heaven the conventional way. When we do, we probably won't notice the glitches."

"So let's go see Frankie, and get this going with, or without, the TV station."

They dressed and brushed their teeth. Mike took the poodles out, and Ruby told Buster the plan.

"Getting anxious to get back to life, are we?" Buster said, in Abdul's voice.

"Aren't you? Do you enjoy being a dog? How do you like the dog food?"

Buster scratched his ear, stood, yawned, and stretched his dog body. "I haven't eaten in days. I guess I should keep Buster's body fed. Bring me a steak from the ramada."

When Mike and the poodles came in, Ruby suggested they get breakfast and bring it back to eat at the cottage. "We can bring a treat to the dogs, too."

"Shall we fly up?"

"You fly up, Mike, and get in line. I need the exercise. I'll jog up and join you."

By the time Ruby joined him in the line, Mike had convinced another man to go to the Rebirth Center. He smiled as the guy loped off, forgetting about breakfast.

"Another notch on my belt. When this show hits the TV waves, there's going to be a stampede."

They reached the food. "Let's get the kids each a steak. You put two on your plate and I'll put one on mine. Do you notice the food aromas? They got that part right."

They flew back to the cottage with loaded plates.

"Don't get used to this, but we're treating the three of you for being such good kids." Ruby cut the meat into bites and put their dishes down.

Sitting on the sofa with their own breakfast, Ruby asked, "What did the guy in line do in his former life?"

"He was a politician. He spent a few months in Life Review, atoning. It was interesting, Ruby. He didn't know he was hurting anyone."

"He *says*. Do you think people in Heaven can lie?"

"I don't know. Tell me a bunch of stuff and put a lie in, and let's see what happens."

She thought for a minute. "I know Duke and Duchess want to go home, but Buster told me he's having too much fun in Heaven. He wants us to tell Abdul he'll stay awhile."

"But what?" Mike asked.

Ruby stared at him. "You didn't hear what I said about Buster?"

"You didn't say anything about Buster."

"Oh-Ho! That answers my question. The rest of the sentences were about Buster not wanting to go home with us. They were lies. The politician was telling the truth."

Mike stopped eating and looked at Ruby. "I wish that was true in life. Just think, no lying in court, no scams, no two-faced politicians. It would be a better world."

"Want to stay?"

"No. I'll take our complicated life, with all its duplicity."

The dogs finished their steak dinners and happily licked their chops.

"Shall we tell the dogs the meat here is plant-based?" Ruby whispered. Mike gave her a quizzical look. "Ya think? It tastes like the real thing to me."

"Let's fly to the station. I'm going to miss flying when we get home," Ruby said.

As they settled to the ground outside the station, Frankie opened the door and motioned them in. "Come look at my new toy. It just arrived."

He was excited, but he spoke in modulated tones. Ruby and Mike looked at each other and shrugged.

"A TV camera," Mike said, somewhat underwhelmed.

"Yes, but it's the hottest camera since the Brownie Bullseye! See this unit on the back? This is a cellular connectivity unit. It allows streaming live to the TV station without the need for a satellite van, which as you know, there are none of here. We're in business!"

"That's great, Frankie because we're hot to trot, too. I've perfected my interview, and it works. Everyone I've talked to runs off to get reborn. This is going to be a success."

"Any reason we can't get started today?" Ruby asked.

"Give me an hour to set up the station to tape the transmissions, and we'll give it its maiden run."

"We should talk to Alice, and make sure she's okay, running the Rebirth Center."

They walked to the Indoctrination cottage and knocked. Alice opened the door. Her ordinarily elaborately coiffed hair was a messy frazzle.

"We're ready to start the interviews," Ruby told her. "Have you noticed more rebirths lately?"

"Today?" she exclaimed. "Can you wait until I find someone to run the facility? I'm doing double duty, and I don't like it. It could be like Grand Central Station, if this thing takes off. It's too much for me."

"Get one of the board members, or train all the board members," Ruby suggested. "They can rotate duty days. If they don't like it, get them to find someone bored enough to move into the Rebirth cottage and be full-time."

"Good idea," Mike said.

"It might work. I'd forgotten I can delegate. Thanks, Ruby." She smiled, saluted, and closed the door.

They walked down the path. "Has it been an hour yet, Mike?"

"Who knows? You know Heaven's the land that time forgot."

Buster met them on the path. "Frankie's ready."

Frankie was indeed, ready. He hoisted the big camera to his shoulder and with a happy grin, stepped out.

They headed for the food ramada. A lone man, walking toward lunch, was their first candidate.

"Hello, sir. Do you have a minute?" Mike said, conversationally.

The man looked at his watchless wrist. "Yea, I guess so. What's up?" He glanced at the camera pointed at him.

"We're starting a 'Man on the Street' interactive interview TV show. Just a short chat for you and your friends to see. What's your name?"

The man glanced nervously at the big camera. "Not interested! Sorry, buddy." He walked, briskly away.

# Chapter 26

"Cut!" Ruby said. Frankie had appointed her as their director.

"I hadn't started filming yet, but that was good," Frankie told her.

"I'm sure we'll get a few 'No Thanks'," Mike said.

A black woman on skates rolled toward them. Her hair streamed out behind her. She'd cut her Heaven-issued pants to make short shorts. She executed a jump, turned mid-air, skated backward, and stopped in front of Mike.

"That was spectacular," Mike exclaimed. "Are you a professional?"

"No. I just picked it up. Why are you blocking the sidewalk?"

"My colleagues and I are interviewing interesting people for a new TV show. You could go back, do a skating routine, roll up, and then I would interview you. Does that sound like fun?"

"Not particularly, but I'll think about it." She skirted around Mike and skated off.

"I think that was a maybe. What am I doing wrong? I had great success talking to people in line."

"I think the camera's intimidating them."

"I have an idea. I'll interview you."

Ruby glanced around. People were coming from every direction. "Okay. Just don't make me look pathetic."

"You couldn't look pathetic, Ruby. Just step up to me."

More were gathering to see what was going on. She silently signaled Frankie to start recording.

"Hello," Mike said in a friendly voice. "May I ask your name?"

"Uh, I think you know it's Ruby." She winked at the onlookers. "This is a demonstration interview, folks. We're a couple. We just want to show you how benign the interview process is. Okay, Mike. Carry on."

"Er, Hello, Ruby," he continued. "Would you be interested in being interviewed for a new TV show called *Now What?* You'll get to see your bit before it airs, and okay, nix, or edit it. Does that sound fair?"

Ruby theatrically batted her eyes at Mike, drawing some giggles from the growing audience.

"Okay," she said. More people stopped to see what was happening.

"Great," Mike enthused. "Are these your dogs?" he pointed to Duke and Duchess.

"Well, yeah."

"So you all landed in Heaven together?"

"Ya think?" she said with a smirk. Some of the people chuckled.

"Ruby, what do you love about Heaven?"

"Everything! What's not to love? It's quiet. No loud garbage trucks, no bossy mothers-in-law, no mortgage, no politicians, or bank accounts to keep track of. And, no illness."

"I know. Now, Ruby," he said with a smile. "What *don't* you like about Heaven?"

A larger crowd gathered. "Can I say I *like* to shop? I like to wear a variety of clothes that *I* picked out. I like to cook and work in the yard." She heard some murmurs from the onlookers.

"And I like going to work."

"Ah. What work did you do?"

"I worked in a pet supply store. Not a career. I was saving up for tuition.

"What would you do with a degree if you went back for another life?"

She looked at the faces that were gathered. They seemed to hang on every word. She pushed her blond curls away from her face to draw out the moment. She imagined some were thinking of their choices.

"I would become a clothes designer," she said slowly. "I'd forgotten that was my dream." She looked into Mike's eyes. "Thank you for helping me remember. I can't imagine why I'd forgotten. Maybe Heaven appeals to my lazy side. But now . . . "
She turned and made her way through the bystanders. Duke and Duchess followed.

"Thank you, Ruby," Mike called. "I'll send for you when it's ready to be viewed."

Mike scoped out the onlookers. They seemed ready to hear someone else's interview. He saw a tall red-haired man standing in the middle of the group.

"Hello, sir. What's your name?" He thrust the microphone toward him.

"Uh, it's Phil."

"Step over here, Phil." Mike extended his hand. People moved aside to let him by. Phil stepped forward to shake Mike's hand.

"Thank you for volunteering to be interviewed for the new TV show, *Now What?* You can come to the TV station to view your segment later. Okay?"

"I guess so," Phil said. His light brown eyes nervously scanned the crowd.

"What do you like about Heaven, Phil?"

"Well, it's relaxing and the food is great. The best part though, is the women." He blushed beet red.

Mike looked at the men and women who were watching. "I see what you mean. Lots of beautiful women here."

To get the conversation back on track, he asked, "What do you like to do, Phil?"

"You mean with women?" Phil repeated his spectacular blush. The bystanders were laughing. At least the men were. Mike felt his own face get warm.

"Do you like to paint or shoot hoops? How do you like to fill your time?"

Phil had a perplexed expression on his face. Mike plunged on.

"What did you do in your former life, Phil?"

The question hung in the air.

Phil compressed his lips and looked at the ground.

"I sold _____."

"I didn't hear that. What did you sell?"

Phil looked uncomfortable. "Uh, I, I can't t-tell you," he stuttered.

"Oh. Okay. Was it a gratifying profession? What did you like about it?"

Phil's eyes darted around. He wanted to bolt, but he was hemmed in. "Look! I did my restitution! What I did was bad. People died. It was a lazy, stupid way to make money. I've learned my lesson. Okay?"

After a pause, Mike asked in a quiet voice, "What would you do if you went back to another life?"

Phil looked into Mike's eyes.

"Don't laugh. I want to be . . . a professional mime."

# Chapter 27

"A mime! Sounds like fun."

Phil mimed as a stooped man, walking with a cane, in a strong wind.

Before Mike could advise Phil to go up to the Rebirth Center, a tall man edged his way through the crowd. He stepped up.

"May I be next?"

"Sure. What's your name?"

"It's Chris."

"Hi, Chris. You look familiar. Have we met before?"

"I doubt it."

Mike scanned the man's black curly hair and handsome, square-jawed face. He was sure he'd seen him.

"You asked that other guy what he liked about Heaven, and I want to say that we've been tricked by the most outrageous scam known to mankind!" He was passionate.

"Tell us what you mean."

Chris turned to the crowd who stared at him with puzzled expressions.

"We've been told this is Heaven! I'm telling you that we're in Hell!"

A curl of Chris's black hair fell to his forehead. Mike's eyes got big. He searched his memory, sure now, he knew who this man was, if he could only recall.

The men and women around them murmured. Some shook their heads no. Others looked confused.

"So Chris, why have you come to this belief?"

"It's not a belief, Mike. It's a reality." Chris spoke calmly now. "We're all prisoners in this parody. We're fed, housed in these identical ticky-tacky houses, given these unimaginative pajamas to wear, and these old-people shoes. We're lulled into complacency by unending good weather, pretty flowers, and worse," his voice rose, "no night, no stars, and no moon. It's all FAKE! Wake up, people! We all drank the Kool-aid! We're goldfish, swimming around mindlessly, in a bowl. I want **out**!"

"What did you do, Chris, in your last life?"

The man's expression went blank. He looked at Mike. "I, I can't remember."

"Take your time. It will come to you."

"I . . . was . . . an actor! Why would I forget that?" he whispered.

"I call it the Heaven effect," Mike said. I guess it makes it easier to accept everything. Would you go into acting again if you had the choice?"

"You bet I would. I just wouldn't . . . show horses."

"Superman!" Mike blurted. "You're Christopher Reeves!" Mike pumped his hand and said, "It's obvious that Heaven doesn't appeal to you. Why don't you go back?"

"Go back? Have you noticed there are no airports? There's no road leading out and even if there was, there's no cars or planes, or even busses! Hell! I would *run* out of here if I knew which direction to run."

"Nobody told you how to go back when you arrived?"

Chris looked confused. Two furrows appeared between his brows. "Go back? What do you mean? As a ghost?"

138

Mike looked out at the crowd. "Were any of you told you could go back to another life when you arrived in Heaven? Raise your hand if you were."

They all looked at each other but nobody raised a hand.

"This is tragic," Mike said. "Heaven is meant to be a rest between lives. Everybody can go back whenever they're ready. There's a cottage by the Orientation Center. It's the Rebirth Center. When you're ready, go up and knock."

"Rebirth?" Chris said. "I would be born as someone different?"

"Yes and no. You would still be you but you would take on the DNA of the new parents you'd be born to. Your essence stays with you, though. You'll grow up with all the basic knowledge and human skills you've accrued throughout all your lifetimes."

Chris stared at Mike.

"How do you know this? Are you an Angel or something?"

Mike, momentarily floored, didn't know what to say.

An answer came to him. "Chris, I've recycled so many times, the Heaven effect no longer affects me." *Don't know how I got by with that lie, but Chris heard me.*

Then Mike noticed Buster sitting in the grass staring at him and lazily scratching behind one ear.

"Thanks," Chris said. "I'm off to the Rebirth Center. Color me gone!"

"Good luck, Superman," people on the sidelines called to him.

"I have time for one more interview. Anybody game?"

"Me," he heard. A woman's hand at the back of the crowd shot up.

People turned and made way for her to get through.

"Oh, it's the skater. I'm glad you changed your mind. What's your name? "

"Cindy," the woman answered. "Everything you told Chris was a lie. There's no such thing as being reborn. That's triple hogwash."

"No, Cindy, it's not a lie, and I can prove it."

She turned to the people listening. All the men believed *her*. After all, she was beautiful with her chocolate coloring and electric green eyes.

"Listen to me," she shouted. "I went up to the so-called Rebirth Center with my friend. He wanted to see for himself if it was bogus. It was! Totally!"

"What happened, Cindy?" Mike prompted.

"I'll *tell* you what happened. He stepped into this circle on the floor, and the rebirth man pressed a button and my friend disappeared. Whoosh! He was vaporized! All that was left were his clothes."

"That's the process, Cindy. It's painless, instant, and without trauma or stress. Your friend is now a fetus floating comfortably in his mother's amniotic cradle. Very soon, he'll be able to suck his thumb, stretch, and make faces."

Cindy still looked skeptical. "I still say you're lying."

"I can prove I'm not lying. I'm going to say something to you, and it will be a lie. Everybody, watch what happens. My name is Mike. I came to Heaven after I dropped a hammer on my big toe. It turned septic and I died."

"That proved nothing! You just mouthed the rest so we'd think you can't lie."

"Okay. I challenge you to do the same. Tell me something and slip a lie into the middle. Everybody, watch what happens."

She turned to the mostly adoring crowd.

"I was the top model with a European model agency. I was shot to death in a bank holdup."

"Did anyone hear what she said?" Mike asked.

"She didn't say anything," a woman said.

"She said something, but it was too quiet for anyone to hear," one man argued.

"What she said was a complete lie," Mike said. "Wasn't it, Cindy? That proves that in Heaven, nobody can tell a lie."

"Well, yeah," she said. "I heard myself, though. Nobody else did?" She looked at the crowd, who were shaking their heads.

"What did you do in your life, Cindy?"

She looked down at the path and then into Mike's face.

"Take your time. It will come to you."

Her shoulders slumped. "Do I have to tell you? Oh, hell, why not? I was a high-priced hooker," she said under her breath.

"Oh, an entertainer," Mike said, congratulating himself for his response. "Was it satisfying? Uh, I mean, what did you like about your work?"

"The money. That was the only thing, except the hours."

"So Cindy, if you went back, would you want to go into the same profession?"

She looked at Mike and turned to the men and women who hung on her words.

"Guess what, folks. I'm not going up to that so-called Rebirth Center and standing on that circle. If you want my advice, don't go. *This* is Heaven."

"But you could go into a different line. You could go to college and learn a profession that made money *and* made you happy."

"Gee, Mike, that sounds like a bundle of fun." She turned and skated off. People's expressions were either shocked or confused.

"Thank you, Cindy," he called. "We'll contact you when we're ready for you to come to the TV station to review your segment."

"End of interviews for today, folks," Mike announced. "I'll post the schedule for the next session."

# Chapter 28

What do you think about Cindy's interview?" Mike asked Frankie and Ruby when they walked back to the TV station.

"It was certainly entertaining." Frankie smiled.

"Yes, but is it the message we want to send?"

"Is it ethical to only televise the messages we agree with?" Ruby asked.

"That's the question, isn't it? Let's sleep on it and decide tomorrow. I'm ready for some chow and some serious shut-eye, but let's agree that it was a good day's work."

They high-fived, and Ruby and Mike strolled toward the food ramada, lost in their thoughts.

"What do you think Abdul would say about airing Cindy?"

"I don't know, but I'm for airing it. She was colorful and articulate. It would show that the program isn't biased. That's a good thing. Right?"

"R-i-g-h-t," Mike drawled. But the mission of the show is to nudge people to realize that Heaven isn't the end of the road.

They joined the line at the ramada. Ruby tapped the shoulder of the man standing in front of her. He turned and looked at her.

"Hi," she said, smiling at the scowling African American. "My name's Ruby. Did you hear about the brand-new TV show? We're looking for people to interview."

His brows shot up. "Why?" he said.

"Why interview? Well, it's a way to hear people's views on what's right and what's wrong with Heaven. I would love to hear what you have to say."

"Why?"

Ruby laughed. "I'm betting that you have some really interesting things to say. What's your name, Why-man?"

"It's," he paused ". . . Oombagallo."

"Great name. The next interview session's happening uh, the next time lunch is being served. We just finished the first interviews, and we want four more for our first show, Oom-er . . ."

He grinned. "You can call me Oom, or you can call me Roy."

Smiling, Ruby turned to Mike. "This is the interviewer. Mike, this is Oom, but you can call him Roy, or you can call him Oombagallo. I've been talking to him about our TV interviews."

Mike smiled. They shook hands. "We've gotten some really interesting answers on the subject. People seem to enjoy sharing their views. We need your perspective, Roy."

"Why?"

"Why? Because everyone's answers have been different. Because everyone in Heaven didn't have the same experience, or the same viewpoint."

"Oh," Roy said. "I thought it was because I'm a black man."

"Actually, Oom, it's because you're standing in front of Ruby, and we talk to everyone we can about this interview opportunity. Let me interview you. I bet you can't even remember your life before Heaven."

"Hm-m-m. Maybe I'll just make something up. Is the truth a requirement?"

"If you lie, no sound will come out of your mouth. It's part of the Heaven effect."

Roy's eyes got big. "No shit?"

"I can't lie. By the way, how'd you get the name Oombagallo? It's very exotic."

"My mother emigrated from Swaziland. That's an African monarchy, with one foot in modern life and one foot in ancient traditions. The king has seven wives. Mom was a very pretty maiden, and she didn't want to risk being wife number eight. But she misses her beautiful country, so when I was born, she named me Oombagallo. My dad, from Atlanta, wanted to name me Roy."

"Roy, nothing I could ask you in an interview, would be as fascinating as what you just said. I can't wait to get you in front of the TV camera. Is it a deal?"

"We'll see. Maybe. Oh, it looks like I'm next for the food line. See ya around, Ruby. Mike."

They looked at each other. "This job gets more fun every day. I love interviewing. I may create something like this when we get back to Denver," Mike said.

Going through the food line, they each added a steak to split among the dogs.

"Shall we eat here or fly back to the cottage?"

"Let's eat here. We might get a chance to talk to someone else." They searched the tables and found a space, next to a group of hungry-eyed women who watched Mike as they sat down.

"Here's to a successful day." Ruby picked up her glass of tea and tipped it to Mike's glass. They clinked and to further establish their relationship, she kissed Mike on the lips. He grinned.

"Are we all set now?"

"Yep. Go for it. Just remember, you're partial to blonds."

He ruffled her curls. "You have nothing to worry about, Blondie."

They tucked into their fish and chips. "Good, huh," Mike said. "Do you notice that we *can* smell the food, Rube?"

"Yes, and I have a theory. You know how nobody ever remembers being in Heaven? My theory is that since the strongest senses for memory recognition are smells, we don't remember Heaven because there are no smells."

"Then why do we smell the food? Doesn't that shoot down your theory?"

"Not at all. No food smells, no appetite. Heaven is a unique experience, but everybody eats, in all their lives."

"I get it. Did anyone ever tell you, you're one smart cookie?"

"Not yet. Are you telling me?"

"Maybe."

She laughed and pinched him on the thigh.

"Time to go to work," Mike said. He turned and spoke to the woman on his left. Her hair was mouse-brown, but Ruby noticed her lashes were thick and upswept, and she knew how to use them. *Whatever,* she thought.

She turned to the man on her right. He had just put his fork down.

"Hi," Ruby said, wishing she had the gift of gab, like Mike. The man turned and looked at her.

"Is everyone in Heaven beautiful?" she blurted. He could be Brad Pitts' twin.

His smile was one degree off of lascivious.

*OhmyGosh, don't smile at me like that. Look away, R. Whatever you do, don't look into those eyes.*

"Exactly what I'm thinking, looking at you," he said.

She gulped. "I'm not coming on to you. My name's Ruby. I was just going to tell you about a new TV show that we're doing

146

interviews for. We need four more for the first airing coming up. People seem to enjoy telling Mike what they like about Heaven and what they don't like." She felt like she was nervously rattling off a spiel. She stopped.

"What's your name again?"

"Ruby. What's yours?"

"Steve. Now, what do I get if I allow you to interview me?"

"You get to tell Mike your views on Heaven. Then, you get to come to the TV station and review your segment. If it's a 'Yay', you'll get to watch yourself on TV. If you decide it's a 'Nay', you'll land on the cutting-room floor, so to speak. How does that sound?"

"Might be fun, but Ruby," he reached over and ran a thumb down her cheek, "if I do it, I want to spend an evening with you. Deal?"

She took a deep breath. "Steve, I'm deeply flattered, but Mike," she put her hand on Mike's back, "might not like for me to cavort with such a devastatingly handsome guy. But we would still be interested in what you have to say . . . please?"

"I'll think about it."

"I'll let you know when and where we'll be setting up. And thank you, Steve, for the compliment. She gave him a peck on the cheek and stood.

"Ready, Mike?"

"Go ahead without me. I'll be down in a bit."

She slid her steak onto his plate and extricated herself from the long bench. She felt Steve's eyes on her as she walked away.

With the green-eyed devil sitting on her shoulder, she looked back at Mike, but he was all eyes for Miss flirty eyelashes.

Strictly business, she told herself. *Nothing to worry about, but he better not be much longer. I'll just sit on this bench, and wait so we can go down together. Oh-oh, here comes Steve.*

# Chapter 29

Steve bee-lined straight to Ruby and sat down beside her. "Waiting for me?" he asked.

"Uh, well . . . yes, as a matter of fact." She searched her mind for something else to say.

He took her hand. So far, so good, she thought.

"Steve, were you a twin?"

"I don't know what you mean."

"Think back, Steve. Do you remember what you did in your life?"

"Make sense, Ruby. Of course I remember my life. I live in a gold cottage six streets down. I've had lots of girlfriends. I like to skateboard, and play poker with my buddies."

"That's your life in Heaven. I mean your life before you came here."

He gave her a confused look. "I don't know what you're talking about, girl."

She looked into his eyes.

"Steve, before Mike and I came to Heaven, we lived in a city called Denver in the United States of America. Everyone here came from somewhere else. They lived there, had jobs, families, and lives. Then, that life ended, and they came here to Heaven. They don't remember until Mike asks them what they did in that life. Think back. Can you tell me anything about yourself, before you came to Heaven?"

He silently stared into space. He turned to her. "Everyone?"

"Well, we haven't talked to everyone, but so far, yes. Everyone. Here's what might have happened, Steve. There's a famous actor where I came from, who looks just like you."

He interrupted. "What's an actor?"

She searched her mind for an explanation. "Does anyone put on plays here? You know, acts out a story with other people, for entertainment?"

He frowned.

"Well, it doesn't matter. It happens where I came from, and this man is one of the most popular actors. Perhaps when his mother gave birth to him, she gave birth to you too, but you were a stillborn twin. So maybe you came to Heaven without having a life first.

"Huh! Is there any way we can confirm that? I'd like to know."

"I don't know, Steve. We could talk to Alice. Want to?"

He thought a moment. "Okay."

They took the path that led to Alice's cottage. Mike quickly caught up with them.

"Hey! What's up?" he said. He took Ruby's hand.

"Oh, hi, Mike. Steve and I are going up to Alice's cottage to ask her about Steve's former life. He can't remember having one."

"No former life? How can that be possible?"

"Let's see what Alice says. I have a theory."

They knocked on Alice's door. She invited them in.

"Alice," Ruby began, do you remember Steve?"

"Who could forget you, Steve? You've come to Heaven many times."

Steve's eyes got big, and then he frowned. "I don't think so, Alice."

"Alice, Steve doesn't remember living a life before Heaven. Is it possible that he didn't have one?"

"Not all babies survive, dears," she said softly. "Things can go wrong, especially with multiple births. Perhaps your mother wasn't close enough to a hospital when you and your brother decided to make your entrances into life. But Steve, you had many lives before your last one was cut short." She sat down beside him. "Take my hand."

He looked at Ruby, shrugged, and took Alice's hand.

"Now, close your eyes. Mine are closed, too."

They were quiet.

"I remember that! It's my dog, Fritz! Is that me?"

"Yes, Steve. You were seven. Sit back and watch."

"That's me in my high-school cap and gown. Oh, look. Mom with the camera. God! I was such a dork!" He was quiet for a while. Then quietly, "Yep. They drafted me."

More quiet time. Mike and Ruby saw a tear trickle down Steve's cheek. He turned loose of Alice's hand, wiped his face, and turned to her.

"That one didn't turn out so good, did it?"

"You had a good childhood and loving parents. Some children don't even get that. Your slate's clean, Steve. Think of what you would like to create in your next life, and when you're ready, go at it with fervor. How do you feel?"

"I don't know. I *do* know I'm going to look at Heaven with different eyes. How long have I been here?"

"It doesn't matter. You can stay until you're ready to go."

"How long, Alice?"

"It's been a little over twenty-seven years."

There was a stunned silence.

"Thank you for this, Ruby and Alice. Mike, I *do* want to be interviewed. Now, if you'll excuse me, I need to go to my *cottage*. I'll be in touch." He grinned, winked at Ruby, and left.

"His interview is going to wake a lot of people to their similar circumstances, isn't it?" Alice commented. "I'm beginning to see the value of this project."

Mike and Ruby were quiet, as they walked to their cottage. Finally, Mike spoke. "You hit pay-dirt with Steve. That was interesting. Who knew Alice could do that?"

"Yeah. Everybody has a story. I'm tired, Mike. I don't know how people get used to no evening, no morning, and no concept of time. I'm going to get cranky any minute now if only there *were* minutes. I want to go home . . . real home."

They were at their seafoam blue cottage, with the seafoam blue flowers. "I used to like seafoam blue," Ruby groused.

They stepped inside. The dogs were ecstatic. Ruby sat on the floor and hugged them. Buster stretched and yawned.

"We're sick of this place, Mom. We want to go home," Duchess whined.

"We're going to make a plan, Duch. Anything is bearable if we're not stuck, so be patient, and we'll wrap this up, and go home soon."

"I'll take them for a romp while you take a nap. Then, we'll sit and plan. Okay?"

"Thanks, Mike. First, I need a kiss." Mike pulled her up from the floor, bent her back, and kissed her, passionately.

"Don't take too long romping with the dogs," she said, a little breathlessly. "You'll find me in the boudoir."

Mike wiggled his brows at her. "You'll probably be asleep."

"Then wake me," Ruby whispered.

# Chapter 30

Mike and Ruby woke when the poodles jumped onto the bed.

"Is it morning?" she asked, groggily.

"The sun's shining," Mike observed.

"Oh, right. Like that means anything in Heaven. I suppose you dogs have an internal clock that says you're hungry and you need to go out."

"Me too," Buster growled. "Someone locked the doggy door."

"Mike, if I take them out, will you fly up and get us breakfasts? I'm not ready to face Heaven yet."

"Deal. What do you fancy, this fine morning, M'lady?"

Ruby looked at Mike. He seemed as cheerful as she was draggy. "*M'lady* fancies a normal life in Denver, but I'll settle for a stack of pancakes with blueberry syrup and a cup of coffee. Let's make a plan this morning."

"Right. Keep your chin up, Ruby. I have some ideas I think you're going to like." That said, Mike pulled her up from the bed, kissed her, and sailed out the door.

"Huh!" Ruby glanced in the mirror. "Fruck it," she said to her tangled, blond mop.

"Come on, Sweeties. Let's go out." She grabbed a handful of poop bags by the kitchen door dispenser and let the anxious dogs out.

Mysteriously, the grass in Heaven always remained green, mowed, and free of weeds. In the corner of each yard, a small, buried, metal unit for waste disposal whisked everything away in a swish. *I'll miss these,* Ruby admitted.

She stretched and began her neglected yoga, while Duke and Duchess rolled in the grass and played, mock biting each other's legs and running in happy circles. Buster snoozed in the sun.

"Breakfast!" Mike called from the back door. He stood aside as the dogs stampeded in.

"Oh boy, steak again!"

"Don't get spoiled, you mutts. When we get home from this vacation, it will be back to kibble."

Mike and Ruby sat at the tiny table and smiled at each other.

"Feeling better?" Mike asked.

"Some. I did my yoga while the poodles played. It felt good, and their joy lifted my gloom." She took a bite of the golden brown pancakes. "M-m-m. Good."

"I make good pancakes too, Ruby. We won't suffer when we go back to Denver. So here's my idea. We interview again today and then air the show in a few days. What did we talk about naming it?"

"I think I mentioned *Now What?*, but maybe *What's Next?* is better. Let's get Frankie's input."

"Okay. After the first showing, we do another week of interviews, and this time we keep our eyes open for a couple of potential interviewers to take my place. I think a woman and a man. If we find one or two people interested, we give them a crash course in the basic intention of the TV show."

"We tell them it's to encourage people to get reborn in order to stem the overpopulation of Heaven?"

Mike frowned.

"You're right. That sounds manipulative. Let's say that in the process of coming to this lovely place, the Heaven effect inadvertently causes people to forget their former life dreams and skills. The interview is to discover who they were before coming here."

"But Mike, what's to keep our new interview recruits from skipping off to the Rebirth Center themselves?"

"I hadn't thought about that." He ate a huge bite of pancake. "In reality, nothing. It's a volunteer position. Maybe we can ask them to vow that, before abandoning the post, they'll recruit and train a new interviewer. It's a fun job. I can print out a list of leading questions to ask."

"Hopefully, Alice and Frankie can keep an eye on things to make sure the intent of the TV show doesn't stray. I think we should stay a few weeks after we hand over the reins to see how it goes. How does a month countdown sound, Mike?"

"Sounds good to me. Let's ask the dogs. Hey, canine crew, family meeting in the living room."

The dogs woke from their morning naps and looked at each other. "Family meeting?" Duchess said after a big yawn. "What's up, Padre?"

"Living room, now!" Mike commanded.

"Okay, okay," Duke growled. "Don't get grouchy. We were napping."

When they were all in the living room and the dogs were more or less at attention, Ruby took the floor.

"We all want to go home. But *Padre* and I came here on a mission, and we want to get it done before we leave. We have a plan. We'll give it a month to make it happen."

"What's a month?" Duchess asked.

"It's the amount of bedtimes when we go see Cathy and you get all pretty to the next time we go see Cathy and get pretty again," Mike told them.

"Oh, that's not very long," Duchess said. "We just start smelling good and then we go get stinky again. We can do that."

"So we all agree that we'll stay here for another month and then go home."

Buster went back to his exciting dream.

"Four accedes and one no-vote. The yays have it." Mike banged his empty mug on the coffee table. "The family meeting is adjourned."

Buster raised his muzzle and gave Mike doggy stink-eye.

At the TV station, Frankie had spliced the interview sequences together.

"You're going to be happy," he enthused. "I did a little narration between the interviews to smooth the transitions. I'll roll it."

Ruby and Mike looked at each other as Frankie cued up the tape. Mike shrugged. After each interview, in a quiet dialog to the TV audience, Frankie praised the person's candor, their surprise former life, or bravery in stepping up. The comments were always positive and supportive and ended in the declaration that a new person had stepped up to be interviewed. "Let's listen," he said to the TV viewers, in a conspiratorial tone.

"Bravo!" Mike called when the tape ended.

"Well done, Frankie," Ruby agreed. "You were great."

Frankie was pleased. "Those people made me think about *my* life before Heaven."

Oh-oh, Ruby thought. This might be so successful at draining Heaven, there won't be anyone left to carry on the show.

"Frankie, would you consider training another person who could take over the station, if you ever decide to get reborn? Your contribution to Heaven is really important, but you have the right to go for another life."

Frankie stared at Ruby. "Leave the TV station?"

"It might be your destiny someday. You wouldn't want to leave Heaven without TV, and I'm certain you don't want to feel like you're stuck here forever."

"I'll think about it," he said.

"How do you like naming the show *What's Next?*" Mike said.

"I like it. Short and provocative. I'll work up an introduction and introduce you. The show will be ready to air the next day, if everybody approves their segment."

"We'll send them up today. Ruby, you were the first interview, so you look at your segment, then Cindy is next. I'll go get Chris and Phil. I'm going to fly to their cottages. See you back at the TV station."

Ruby thought of Cindy and then took to the air. She descended to a pale purple cottage. Lavender flowers edged the walk. Ruby knocked.

"Yeah?" Cindy said as she opened the door. She wore blue pants and a yellow top, cut down into scanty versions of the otherwise sedate garments.

"Hi Cindy, I'm Ruby. Would you like to review your TV interview before we air it? If this is a good time, we could go up together."

"What if I don't approve it?"

"It will end up on the cutting-room floor."

Cindy frowned. "Is there a do-over option?"

"Absolutely," Ruby said. "You can reinterview each week if you want."

"I want to. Run it, as is. Mike can interview me today, and I'll tell him what I know."

# Chapter 31

Ruby and Mike landed at the TV station seconds apart. "How'd you do?" Mike asked.

"Cindy said to run it, but she wants to interview again today. She said she's been thinking. I told her we would be at the food ramada. Where are Phil and Chris?"

Phil's coming up soon, and Chris already rebirthed. So we can run his. We only have one segment to review. Oh, here he is now."

Phil mimed making his way along a glass wall, and then, peering around the edge, pantomimed seeing Ruby and Mike and spread an oversized smile on his face. They laughed and clapped.

"You've been practicing," Mike said. "Bravo!"

"Can I go up to the Rebirth Center? I'm ready to shuffle off this immortal coil."

"Do you want to review your interview first?" Ruby asked.

"Naw. That was amateur hour. I'm outta here. Now!"

"Good luck, Phil. You know you'll get born in nine months and grow up before hitting the stage. Right?"

"Sure, Mike. I'll have all those years to perfect my craft. Toodle-oo!"

Mike and Ruby watched Phil skip up the path.

"This is working better that we thought."

They went into the station and told Frankie the good news. "We're ready to do more interviews as soon as you can set up."

"Give me a half-hour and meet me back here," he said. "We'll go down together."

"Like we'll know when a half-hour is up," Ruby groused as they walked to Alice's cottage.

"Right, but nobody else knows either," Mike reminded her. "So nobody gets uptight about timeliness."

Alice was coming out of the Rebirth Center as they got there. Her hair was a wild tangle and her shirt was inside-out.

"Just the people I wanted to see," she said. "All the board members have rebirthed themselves. I'm doing double duty, receiving *and* sending! Back in the good old days, I could have handled it, but now that there are so many rebirths and a flood of admittances, I'm in over my head! I know you two are waking our residents up to their future dreams but I don't know what's happening on Earth! Something catastrophic."

"Let's go in, and while I make a pot of tea, you can get yourself organized," Ruby proposed. "We'll put our heads together and come up with a plan, okay?"

Alice gave her a grateful smile. "Do I have time to shower?"

"As you know, time in Heaven is elastic, Alice. Come back out when you're calm and collected. Meanwhile, Mike and I will put on our thinking caps."

When they heard the shower running, Mike said, "We'll ask Buster what's happening on Earth." They heard a bark at the door. Ruby let him in.

"Quick, Buster. Do you know what's driving the flood of new entrants to Heaven?"

"From time immemorial," the little brown dog quoted, in an un-dog-like manner, "civilization has suffered from bouts of pestilence, war, death, and famine." He paused. "Take your pick."

You're no help, Buster. I guess it doesn't matter. We need to think of a way to streamline the entry and exit process."

Alice walked into the room, braiding her long honey-gold hair. "Can't streamline the entry process. Remember, the person and I need to see their life story, and sometimes, retribution needs to happen before they can be released into Heaven."

"Okay," Mike said. "That leaves the Rebirth Center. Does someone need to be there when a person wants to do the deed?"

"I'll pour the tea while we ponder that." Ruby came back with three cups of steaming tea. She set the tray down on the coffee table. "I have an idea. We could have a Take a Ticket dispenser at the door and a sign saying: Now Serving Number __. There could be instructions inside. It's a simple process, isn't it, Alice?"

"Just stand on the twinkling circle and pull the lever."

"Alice, is there a way to let people leave Heaven without feeling like they're flushing themselves down a toilet?"

"I never thought about it that way, but you have a point."

They sipped their tea, lost in thought until Ruby said, "We're supposed to meet Frankie at the TV station. Let's think about it and reconvene later."

Frankie was ready to set up for another interview session. They strolled down the path, carrying mics, cords, and the large portable camera. Ruby told him about their conversation with Alice.

"I have a suggestion about the exit method. Instead of the flush lever, I can rig it so when they step on the twinkling circle, it's automatic. No lever, no button, no cord to pull. I can even have it play *On The Road Again* or *Happy Trails To You.*"

"Good suggestion, Frankie. I'll present it to Alice."

They chose a location to begin the interviews, close enough to the diners to attract attention and far away enough to not interfere with conversations. Ruby stuck a signpost into the flower bed with a sign she had prepared: YOU ARE INVITED TO JOIN AND PARTICIPATE IN INTERVIEWS FOR THE NEW TV SHOW, WHAT'S NEXT? COME GIVE US YOUR THOUGHTS. IT'S FUN!

A few people that had finished eating, straggled up.

"Welcome to the *What's Next?* TV interview. It just takes a few minutes, and after you review your segment, you can decide if we run it on the show or not. It's fun, and you get to tell us how you feel about your life in Heaven. Who's game?"

Cindy, from the day before, shouted, "Me! Me!" She wove through the growing group of curious men and women.

"Hi Cindy," Mike said warmly. "I remember your interview. You were sure that rebirthing wasn't real. You assured everybody that Heaven was the end of the line. Right?"

"But that was then."

She'd cut out a peek-a-boo circle on each hip of her cut-down pants. Mike adjusted the height of his eyebrows.

"Are you here to back up your former claims?" He handed her a microphone.

She took it and turned to the crowd. "My last life was not good for me. So Heaven felt like, well . . . Heaven. Nothing harsh, no wrong life choices, no bad people, no STDs. I was set. But Mike, here," she turned and looked at him, "reminded me what I'd conveniently forgotten. I was angry when he suggested I could have another chance for a better life. Why? I thought. *This* is my good life."

She continued, "But I couldn't stop thinking about it. I woke up to another perfect day, dressed in my Heavenly clothes, put on my Heavenly roller skates, and went to the food ramada for

162

another Heavenly breakfast. I flirted with a very cute guy, and we made a date. As I skated away, I thought, this is exactly what I did yesterday and the day before, and yes, even the day before that."

"So, Cindy, did you have a revelation?" Mike asked.

"If that means I had a sudden realization that I wanted something different, then yes. I've had exactly the right amount of Heaven, and now I want to try a new life." She paused. "Today, if that's possible."

Mike smiled. "Thanks, Cindy for sharing your story. Go for it!"

The crowd, which had doubled, clapped hesitantly. Cindy turned and waved. She threw them kisses and skated off to see Alice. The men's eyes followed her shapely derriere as she skated up the hill. There was a collective sigh.

"Well, that was fun," Mike said. "Who wants to tell our TV audience what you love and *don't* love about Heaven? Oh, I see Oombagallo."

"You can call me Roy, Mike."

"Step up, Roy. I'm glad to see you. As I remember from our conversation in the dinner line, you have recollections about your life. What was your profession?"

"I was a music teacher at a high school. I liked it. And then, I was accused of a murder I didn't commit. I was convicted and put on death row. I'm not going back if I have to be a black man again. Can you help me, Mike?"

Mike didn't know what to say. *I'm in over my head. What can I possibly suggest to help this man?* He looked at Ruby. She shrugged. Then he caught sight of Buster, looking at him, pointedly.

"Uh, Roy, I don't know whether you would be reborn as a black man or not, but in either uh, racial, uh, manifestation . . ."

He was interrupted by someone who spoke to them from the audience.

# Chapter 32

"I can answer your question," came a soft voice from the crowd. Everyone turned to look.

Mike smiled at the Native American woman. "Please come up and introduce yourself."

She lowered her dark eyes and stepped through the group. Mike towered over her. He gave her the mic and said, "What's your name?"

"It's Annie Kee. I'm Navajo." Her black hair was pulled into a double knot at the back of her head. "I've been reborn many times, and . . . I remember my lives."

"That's unusual, isn't it Annie? Most don't even remember their last life. You said you can answer Roy's question. Is that because you learned information from your reincarnations?"

"Yes," she said.

"Can you tell us?" Mike urged.

She looked down at Roy's feet. She spoke quietly in the distinctive cadence of her tribe. "You had a life that ended bad. You're afraid it will happen again."

"It happened because I'm black. I don't want to be a black man again."

"You were a good man. You will have a good life when you go again. I know this. People who did bad things have a difficult new life because they need to learn, usually the hard way. Some cultures call it *Karma*. Don't be afraid, Roy."

"Will I be born black?" he asked.

"I was born one hundred lives that I remember. I was tribal in all but one. I was curious about living as a white woman. But in that life, I was so out of place, I wanted to die. When I looked at my people from that perspective, I knew I wanted to be reborn to my tribe so I could help."

"What can just one black man do, though?"

"You could become a lawyer and be an advocate for wrongly accused black men and women. You could start an agency that gets innocent black men and women out of prison. You could become a journalist who writes of injustices and informs the public. Choose something you're passionate about. Devote your life to it."

"I could do that?"

Annie smiled. "Set your mind on a goal, Roy. Now. Before you get reborn. Want it with all your heart. Dream of how it will feel to succeed. How much you will help people like you. You *can* do it. Know that."

Roy's eyes got big. "I . . . I don't know what to say." He closed his eyes. A silence fell that no one seemed willing to break. Ruby stepped up to Roy and quietly led the overwhelmed man to a bench.

Mike counted to five and then turned to the woman.

"What else can you tell us from your experiences, Annie?"

"Learn everything you can and be kind even when nobody is looking. Give your things that you don't need away. Treat women better than you treat yourself." She smiled up at Mike. "I just thought of that. I like it."

"I like it too. Can you tell us about your last life?"

"I moved off the res and went to school to be a nurse. When I went back to my village, I married. He was a good man, but

166

he had many problems. It's hard to be a Navajo man." She looked into the people's eyes, who had gathered to listen.

"When you don't learn your life's lesson before you die, you get a new chance in the next life to do the right thing. But in each life, the lesson gets harder. I know this."

"So it's about learning to be a better person. What happens when you learn all the lessons, Annie?"

"I don't know. I'm not there yet."

"You've been in Heaven lots of times. What do you like, and what do you *not* like?" Mike asked.

She tipped her head and looked at Mike out of the corners of her dark eyes. "I know why you're here, Mike. Good job. There's nothing not to like. It's a rest stop. When I'm rested, I go on."

"I have a question for Annie," came a voice from the crowd."

"Come on up, please. Annie, do you mind?"

"No," she said simply.

The woman had an abundance of brown curls and large brown eyes.

"My name's Becky. I'm the high-school girl who was murdered. I'd like to know what life lesson I'm supposed to learn from that. And another thing, Annie. Who's the judge? Is it God or Allah or Jesus or Buddha?"

"I don't know everything, Becky. I believe there isn't a single Creator but that we are all part of that manifestation. That makes us our own judge. Each of us must have their own belief. That is mine."

"Huh. But why did I get murdered?"

"I don't know. Maybe a lesson to learn from a previous life. Maybe not."

Becky's eyes drifted into the distance in an unfocused gaze. "Maybe," she said softly.

"I have a question, Annie." Mike leaned down and whispered in her ear. She looked at her feet and then looked up at Mike. "You want to know the last life lesson I learned?"

"Yes, if you want to tell us."

"Don't take shit from anyone," she said. Although she spoke quietly, it seemed that everyone heard her. They murmured to each other. Annie smiled.

"Thank you, Annie. That's a valuable lesson."

Someone in the crowd clapped, and soon, all were clapping. Annie crooked her finger, drawing Mike down.

"Do you want some help?" she said quietly.

"I'll see you at Alice's cottage after the interviews," he said.

"Well," Mike said into the mic. "We have time for one more interview. Anyone have something to get off their chest?"

A man shouted from the back of the audience. "When we get reborn, how are we supposed to learn the lesson if we can't remember our past life?" His voice bordered on belligerent.

"We were just given a clue about that from Annie. Come up and I'll give you the mic."

The man might have just stepped out of a Viking saga. His red hair was wild and rough. He stood well over six feet tall and looked like a bodybuilder with huge arms and a neck like a tree trunk.

"Hi. I'm Mike. Tell us your name."

The man took the microphone and looked down at Mike. "It's Percy." He glared, daring anyone to snicker.

The crowd stood perfectly silent.

"So how do we know what our new life lesson is, since we don't remember our past life? Is that about right, Percy?"

168

"Yeah. We don't even remember being in Heaven. I spent time in the slammer. A lot of time. I don't want to do that again."

"I can imagine. And when you arrived here, you had some restitution to do?"

"Yeah. A bunch of 'um."

"You won't be the same man when you go back though, will you?"

"No, but I'll still be me, right?"

"You, but wiser and more peaceful. Is that what you want?"

"Yeah, I guess. And more handsome. Can I get that?"

"What you *can* get, according to Annie, is another chance to pass the tests that you failed in your last life. Maybe you'll be tempted in some similar way. Think you'll fall for it again, Percy?"

"It seemed so easy. I was smarter than everybody! But . . . I was the one who got sent to prison!"

"Because of the temptation?" Mike asked.

The man frowned and glared at Mike. "Shit if I know," he finally said. "Who's doing this to me?"

"I think what Annie inferred, is that you did it to yourself. If we're our own judges, maybe we're also our own guidance counselor."

Percy scowled. "I'm smarter than to send myself to prison three times," he snarled. He turned and stalked off.

# Chapter 33

On their way back to the cottage after the wrap-up, Ruby talked excitedly.

"Annie was great! She's wise and a font of valuable information! Did you hear how she counseled Roy? That was perfect! Mike, this means we can leave right away after we turn the interviews over to Annie."

"Whoa, Ruby. Not so fast. I haven't even talked to her yet. We don't know if she would want to do that."

"That's why we need to talk to her. Let's go now."

"Slow down, Ruby. We don't want to bowl her over. Besides, we need to feed the dogs and I'm bushed."

"Mike, we have the perfect person to take over so we can go home and you're dragging your feet. Fine! Go take a nap. I'll feed the dogs. Then I'll decide what *I'm* going to do."

Mike shook his head, turned, and walked into their cottage, rather than reply with what could never be the right response.

"It's kibble tonight, boys and girl. Can't eat steak every night."

Duchess gobbled kibble from her bowl like it was a speed contest with Duke.

Buster sniffed at the contents of his bowl, took one kibble out, chewed it extensively, and then took another. He looked at the behavior of the two poodles with unveiled disdain.

"You two are animals," he said.

At the dinner ramada, Ruby scanned the tables. "Annie's not here. Shoot!"

"I've been thinking about your idea that she could take over the interviews," Mike said. "What I've seen of her, she's a bit retiring to be the front person."

"I disagree. I think you're having too much fun being the big handsome television star. You don't *want* to go home. Well, I do!"

Mike felt stung by her accusation, but the line had reached the food so rather than rise to her challenge, he loaded macaroni and cheese, a Greek salad, and garlic toast onto his tray. He scanned the available tables for two empty seats.

"See those two spaces in the far corner?" Mike asked. "Look okay to you?"

Ruby picked up her tray and headed for a single space. Mike shook his head and made his way to the table he'd pointed out. He picked at his food while he puzzled over Ruby's sudden insistence that they abandon their mission. Heaven wasn't the place for a big noisy disagreement. He was between a rock and a hard place and felt he couldn't walk away from what they had started without a good replacement.

"Hey, man, aren't you the dude who's on that TV show?"

Mike wasn't in the mood to schmooze with his table mates but he turned and said, "Yeah, that's me. You've watched the show. Did you like it?"

"At first, I thought it was dumb, but somehow, it hooked me. Now, I watch every one."

"Thanks. What's your name?"

"Call me Bunny, like Bunny Wailer, 'cause I love reggae."

Bunny had white-guy dreds but with his shirt cut into a skimpy undershirt style, he looked more like a surf bum, than a Rastafarian.

"Good to meet you Bunny, I'm Mike. Would you like to be interviewed tomorrow afternoon?"

"Oh wow! Hear that, Marley?" He turned to his friend. "I'm going to be interviewed for *What's Next?* tomorrow."

Marley stopped mid-bite. "Cool! Can I be on it too?" His bid for reggae distinction was a long ponytail of dark blond hair and cut-offs. He had penned *Rasta,* accompanied by musical notes across the front of his shirt.

"I'd like that. You could interview right after Bunny."

The friends grinned and high-fived each other. "What time?" Bunny asked.

"After lunch, you'll see me and Frankie set up a ways from the ramada. Bunny, tell me what you liked about the show."

"Everything, Man. I like hearing them remember what they did in their life. Made me think of what I did in mine. It wasn't that interesting but I know what I'm going to do in my next one."

"Don't tell me now, Bunny. Save it for tomorrow. That's the part I like too. That, and seeing them excited about leaving Heaven and going for their next adventure."

Bunny became quiet. Mike could see uncertainty bloom on his face.

He stood and picked up his tray. "See you both tomorrow. You're going to make the show one of the best. Everybody's going to love you guys."

Mike scanned the tables, but Ruby had gone. He sighed. I need to talk to . . . someone about this, but who? He thought. He imagined sitting down with Alice but headed to the TV station to talk to Frankie.

173

When he stepped into the station, Frankie was putting on a reel of *I Love Lucy*.

"Hi, Mike. You look a little dejected. Anything I can help with?"

"Maybe. Can you keep a big secret?"

Frankie set the reel in motion and came over to Mike with a serious look. "I have a couple of beers on ice. Everything's easier when you have a beer in your hand."

"Beer? I thought there wasn't any alcohol in Heaven."

"*My* secret. There are ways if you're devious. Have a seat. I'll be right back."

With a cold beer in his hand, Mike raised his bottle to Frankie. They tapped and took a long swig.

"I can't tell you how good this tastes! It feels like it's been a year since I drank a beer, and yet, I've only been here in Heaven . . . who knows how long?"

He felt the knotted muscles in his neck and shoulders relax. After rolling his head in a circle and flexing his shoulders, he gave his friend a long look. "You can never tell anyone what I'm about to say."

Frankie nodded.

"Ruby and I didn't die to come to Heaven." Frankie's brows shot up, but he didn't comment.

"Ruby was going to be an Angel for two weeks. Don't ask how that came about, but that's how I met her. Anyhow, she had a metaphysical mentor through that episode, and when she returned to what I'll call civilian life, she told her mentor that she would occasionally consider special assignments."

Mike took a sip of his beer and assessed Frankie's expression, to see how he accepted this information.

"Okay so far?" he asked.

Frankie took a drag on his beer and said, "Go on."

"The mentor told us that people came to Heaven and stayed, which created overcrowding and caused the birth rate on the planet to dip alarmingly low. He asked if Ruby would go to Heaven and solve the problem."

"But you didn't need to die first?"

"I'll get to that. I didn't want her to go. I bucked and groused, but Ruby's her own person so I said she should go and I'd stay in Denver with the dogs. We went to bed that night and woke up here. All five of us, including Buster."

Frankie took off his glasses, cleaned them on his shirt tail, and took a sip of his beer. Mike waited.

"*That's* why you created the TV show and called it *What's Next?* So what's the problem? It seems like you've been successful. People like the show, and they're lining up to be reborn in every village in Heaven."

"The problem is that now, as in *right now*, Ruby wants to go home. I can't go until I find someone who wants to do the interviews and will be good at it. That's not going to happen overnight."

"Have you asked Ruby why she needs to go now?" Frankie asked.

"No. She's so combative, she accused me of not wanting to give up my exalted position of Grand PooBoo of Heaven TV. She wouldn't sit with me at lunch today."

"Hmm. You have interviews tomorrow, and the show airs in the evening. How about this? At the end of the show, you announce the call for tryouts to be the new interviewer. In fact, if you like the idea, let's pre-record it now."

Mike looked at Frankie. "You. Are. A. Genius. I love it! This should cheer Ruby up and give us a few days to see how it works. Frankie, I could kiss you! Let's record it now."

They clinked bottles. Frankie set up the camera, and Mike cleared his throat, hid the beer, and said, "Roll it."

He hurried back to the cottage, anxious to give Ruby the good news. Maybe she'll tell me why the sudden need to get back to Denver, he thought.

He found her sitting in the backyard with the dogs. He wished he'd hit Frankie up for two more beers. He sat down beside her on the grass.

"Hi, Sweetheart. I have good news."

She faced him, hooking her hair behind an ear. She'd been crying. "We're leaving?"

Mike put his arm around her. "Hopefully, in a couple of days. Frankie shot me putting out a call for interviewer tryouts to air after the show tomorrow. Men and women can come to the television station, and Frankie will record them." He looked closely at Ruby. "What do you think?"

"Two days? For sure?"

"You, Frankie, and I will judge the applicants. It'll be fun. We'll probably get a bunch of good ones. Then, you, I, and the dogs will become dots on the horizon." He grinned. "If only there *was* a horizon."

Ruby put her arms around Mike and her face into his chest. In a muffled voice, she said, "I can wait a couple of days, but no longer."

They sat snuggled together, watching the dogs play. "If we were home, we'd be watching the sunset. I miss Denver, Mike."

"I do too. We'll be there soon. Meanwhile, let's make these last days in Heaven fun . . . and fulfilling."

"Okay . . . starting right now. Last one in bed's a knuckle-dragger!"

# Chapter 34

"Well, that wraps up this session, folks," Mike said. "Thanks for being a part of the interviews for *What's Next?* Tomorrow we'll be back here. Be thinking of what you would like to declare, question, or complain about." Mike waved and clicked off the microphone.

There was a smattering of applause, and people started to wander away. Leaving two people still standing. The woman flashed a wide smile from a face that was pretty in a lantern-jawed way.

"Hi! I'm Marcy. We'd like to be interviewed for *What's Next?* We have a funny story to tell about . . . "

"Marcy, I haven't talked to anyone who thinks their death was funny. Frankie, do you want to record this? Might be good."

"This is my boyfriend, Sammy," she said. "He was a dive master at a sky diving facility outside of Albuquerque. That's in New Mexico. After we dated for a few months he talked me into diving with him."

Ruby's eyes got big. "Your chute didn't open?"

"Bingo. But, he had an emergency chute, so we weren't worried. We thought it was hilarious, didn't we, Samuel?"

"Well, yes, but you're not going to tell the whole thing are you?"

"Why not? We're in Heaven. Nobody's going to judge us here, are they Ruby?"

"Not a soul, Sammy. Heaven is judgment-free. Why don't you tell your version?"

People starting to wander off, returned, sensing another bit of entertainment coming up.

Sammy's face had turned a rosy pink.

"I, I d-don't think . . . "

"We were still a long way from the ground," Marcy stated. "Sammy's conveniently on top of me, right? I just unzipped my jeans, and the rush of air flew them off into the wild blue yonder. So we did it. Talk about a thrill! We were having so much fun we didn't notice the ground coming up."

"Splat?" Ruby asked.

"We didn't suffer. We woke up here. Not a bad way to go, huh? They probably had to use the jaws of life to get us separated." She grinned at Sammy.

"I'm guessing it didn't do Sammy's standing as a dive master any good," Ruby offered.

"No, but it was the best ever! Try it someday. The sex, not the splat." She looked at Mike. "Is this handsome guy your squeeze?"

Mike's eyebrows shot up.

"I guess you could say we're each other's squeeze," he answered. "Look, we missed lunch doing our TV gig. Would you like to sit with us while we grab a bite?"

"I'm starving," Sammy said. "We accept!"

"Sammy's always hungry. Is this place open twenty-four hours? I won't be able to pry him away. Is it expensive? My credit card flew away with my jeans."

"Come on. The line's short, for once. We'll give you the orientation lecture when we sit down. You're going to love Heaven," Mike told them.

"What's good?" Sammy asked as they picked up their trays. "This reminds me of my school days."

"The food won't remind you of cafeteria fare. This is Heaven. Everything here is the gold standard."

They loaded food as they talked. Sammy's tray couldn't accommodate another dish. He looked embarrassed.

"I took too much food. I'm hungry, but I can't eat all this. What should I do, Mike?"

Mike laughed. "I did the same thing the first time I went through the line. Don't worry about it. Remember, this is Heaven."

"Next question, Mike. When do I pay for all this? Do I run a tab?"

"I see a table for four. Let's eat first. It's not complicated."

Ruby and Marcy joined them. Marcy had chosen crab legs, buttered yams, and creamy coleslaw. Sammy had piled on a T-bone steak, pork ribs, scallop potatoes, and three desserts.

It was quiet as they enjoyed their food.

"I'll tell you," Marcy commented. "Dying and going to Heaven makes you hungry."

"Did you get assigned a cottage yet?" Ruby asked.

"Alice told us to come up after lunch, and she would take us to our place. Ruby, are we going to need to take out a loan? Sammy and I are flat, she grinned at the pun, broke."

"Here's the good news, guys. *Everything* in Heaven is free! No monetary system. On the other hand, there are no cars, no night clubs, no dive bars, no movie theaters, no hospitals or doctors, and you can't get pregnant or ill. Because there's nothing to buy, nobody needs a job."

Sammy ate on through Ruby's monologue, but Marcy stopped and stared at her.

"What does everyone do to keep from dying of boredom?"

"From what I've seen, they make friends, flirt, skate, and ride bicycles. Anything they can manage within the parameters of Heaven. You and Sammy are lucky because you have each other. Oh, and they have lots of sex."

Mike continued the narrative. "There's no work to do because everything's done for you. Did you watch the interviews for the TV show?"

"We caught the end."

"I'll conduct another interview session tomorrow after the lunch crowd. The show airs tomorrow evening. I can't tell you when, because there are no clocks. It comes on when you turn on your TV. Don't ask me how. Ruby says it's the Heaven effect. There's no sun to go down, the grass stays mowed, and your clothes are in your closet, laundered and ironed each morning, if there *was* a morning. Nobody wears underwear, and believe it or not, you'll get accustomed to it."

Marcy and Sammy stopped eating. They stared at Mike.

"Anyway, we're looking for new interviewers for the sessions. If either of you would like to try out, come to the TV station. It's easy. All you need is to enjoy talking to people."

Mike told them how to find the station, and to tell Frankie they were there to try out for the interviewer position.

Marcy and Sammy looked at each other. "Let's do it after we see our absolutely free cottage!" They left to find Alice.

"Interesting people, huh, Ruby."

"We meet all types in Heaven."

"Let's take the dogs for a walk before bedtime."

The next day, after breakfast, Ruby and Mike walked hand-in-hand to the station to preview the evening's tryouts. Frankie met them with a big grin on his face.

"We have the first *two* new prospective interviewers!" he told them. "I have them on tape. If you approve, we can have them take a turn this afternoon for a test drive under fire. See if they really have the guts."

They watched the taped tryouts. The first one was Marcy. Frankie played the role of a reluctant subject. She drew him out with her charm and exuberance, and soon he was joining her lead in the fake interview, telling outrageous episodes of his former failures. They laughed.

"Here's Sammy's."

For his trial interview, Frankie played a bitter interviewee with something to get off his chest. Sammy sympathized and asked what his former life was about. Frankie chronicled a list of disappointments and failures of others.

Mike said, "How's he going to pull this off without alienating this kind of person?"

"Just wait," Frankie said.

"Are you going back?" Sammy asked Frankie, who played the beaten man.

"I hated it there. Why should I go back?"

"Because you've seen one side, so now you can go back, and be the shining example of the other side of that coin. You *are* that man, Frankie, because you know exactly how to do it!"

The tape ended. Ruby and Mike looked at each other.

"He had an answer to the hardest kind of interview," Mike said. "I'm okay with these two."

"Me too," Ruby said. She turned away and swiped tears from her eyes.

That afternoon, after the interviews, Mike invited Marcy to try her hand at interviewing. People stood back, not volunteering to be her first subject. She coaxed a man up with her sparkle, and they had a fun exchange. He vowed to get reborn if she would go with him.

Marcy looked over the crowd and picked Sammy to try his hand at interviewing. He had an easier time than he'd had with Frankie. When he finished with the feisty woman, who'd mostly flirted, he looked over the gathering and saw the Native American woman.

"How about you, young lady? Would you like to be interviewed?"

She made her way up to Sammy. "You're doing a good job, Samuel," she said quietly, "but if someone asks a question that you can't answer, I'll be your reference go-to. I've lived hundreds of lives, and I remember everything. Does that sound okay?"

Sammy was speechless. Then he smiled. "You are a treasure . . . what's your name?"

"It's Annie."

"Annie, you just helped me make up my mind."

# Chapter 35

"We're done, Mike! We can go back to the cottage, gather up the dogs, and click our heels together. We'll wake up in Denver! Yahoo!"

"One more day, Ruby. We need to watch one more interview session, just to make sure Marcy and Sammy know to steer people toward rebirth."

Ruby was quiet as she trudged along. Mike took her hand.

"Okay, Ruby?" She didn't answer.

"Look Babe, I don't know if we've been here a week, or a month, because this crazy place has no sense of time passed, but we came here to do a job for your friend Abdul, or actually, for humanity. We came voluntarily, and before we punch out, shouldn't we be sure we've left the job in good hands?"

"And if *you* think we haven't, then what will *you* want to do?" she asked.

Mike knew it was a loaded question. He wisely answered with another question.

"What would you want to do?"

"You know what I want, Mike. Frankie would fix the problem. We don't need to babysit Heaven personally 'til the end of time. Go up to Frankie's now, and remind him to prompt the current interviewer to talk up getting people back to life. You can tell him goodbye and give him a big ol' man hug. Okay?"

"Tell me why you want to go home now, and I'll do it."

"Do it, Mike, and then I'll tell you why I want to go home now."

"Really?" Mike asked.

"Really. And then you'll understand, I promise."

They stood, assessing each other for a few seconds. Mike turned and walked out of the door. "See you in a bit," he called.

"Tell him goodbye for me," she called back.

When Mike got back to the seafoam blue cottage they'd called home for an undetermined amount of time, he felt a wave of lightheartedness.

"Goodbye, blue geraniums. I'm going back where flowers look real."

He stepped into the front door. "Honey," he called. "I'm home."

Silence. It felt ominous.

"Ruby! Duke! Duchess!"

There was no response. He headed for the bedroom, Ruby had labeled the inside of an organ.

It was as empty as the rest of the cottage, but there was writing on the pillowcase.

*I'm in Denver with the dogs, Mike. If you're ready to come home, tap your heels together three times, and say: There's no place like home. It's corny but it's what we set up.*

*LOVE,*

*Ruby*

When Ruby opened her eyes the next morning, Mike was beside her in the big, log bed. He rose on one elbow and looked down at her.

"I told Frankie goodbye. Our deal was if I did that, you would tell me why it was so important to you to come home. We're home. Tell me, my little homing pigeon."

"Um . . . well, uh-I don't quite know how to . . . "

"You're not leaving me, are you?" Mike blurted.

"Oh, no! Just the opposite. Mike, how do you feel about . . . "

"Are you asking me to marry you?" His voice hit a new octave, with the word, 'marry'.

"Not directly, but if you wanted to, it would give our baby legitimacy."

"Our WHAT?"

"Our baby, Mike. We're going to be parents. That's why I wanted to come home. I was worried about being pregnant in Heaven."

Mike flopped back on his pillow, his eyes unfocused on the ceiling.

"Are you upset?" Ruby asked.

He rolled over and drew her to him. "Not at all. I'm thrilled, I think. I just never . . . do you think I could be a good father?"

"If I didn't think you'd be a good father, Mike, I wouldn't be here when you showed up. I'd be far away, and you would never know you'd fathered a child."

"I fathered a child," Mike said. "We should get married!"

"No."

"What do you mean, no? Kind of late to say no isn't it, with our baby on the way?"

"Mike, there's no 'should' in front of the words, get married. We didn't deliberately create a baby but he, or she, won't care if

185

we're married or not. So the only reason to get married is if we *want* to. Not because we should. So let's just think about it for a while. Okay?"

"Do you love me?" Mike asked.

"With all my heart."

The long silence that followed, confused Ruby, and then infuriated her. She threw the covers off and scrambled from the high bed. Duke and Duchess watched the drama unfold from the bedroom doorway. "Oh-oh," Duchess said.

Buster, sleeping on the foot of the bed, woke, stretched, and said, "Don't worry mutts." He went back to sleep.

"While you grapple with whatever you're grappling with," Ruby spat, "I'm going to pack up and get out of your life!"

"Oh no, you're not!" He grabbed her hand and slid off the bed. "Not until you answer one question."

He sank to one knee. Ruby's eyes got big, and then . . . she giggled.

Mike frowned. "I'm being . . ." he grinned, "terribly romantic!" He started laughing. "You're wrecking my . . . " He couldn't finish. They laughed until tears ran down their cheeks. Ruby sank to her knees in front of Mike. They hugged and finally toppled over onto the sheepskin rug.

"I love you, Ruby," he gasped. "I want us to spend the rest of our lives laughing together. Whether you marry me or not." He paused and hiccupped, sending them both into more laughter.

Finally, Mike caught his breath. "Ruby Louise, dammit, would you *please* just say yes!"

# PART 2

# Chapter 36

The front door banged open. "Honey, I'm home, and guess what!"

"You got the job!" Ruby squealed. She stepped out of the office where she'd been surfing the Internet.

Mike threw his arms around her and swung her in a circle.

"Of course you did! They were thrilled to get you back on the team. What about the other thing?"

"They're considering it. They'll take it up with upper management, but they didn't shoot it down . . . yet. I proposed it as an add-on at the end of the hard news segment. Man on the street's opinion of the local current events. We bandied it around enough that I got the feeling they were interested."

The sparkle in Mike's eyes and the big grin on his face made Ruby want to twirl like the dogs when they were excited. She had news too, and she knew the timing to tell him would be tricky, considering his protectiveness about her pregnancy. She was two months along, and according to her gynecologist, she was as healthy as a horse.

"I'm fixing a celebration candlelight dinner with champagne for you, and for me, electrolyte water. The prime rib's in the oven, and the spuds are cooked and waiting for the skillet. Get into your comfy duds. Let's pop the cork!"

Ruby was equally excited and apprehensive of Mike's reaction to the new metaphysical opportunity Abdul had just offered her. But she told herself it wasn't as extreme as going to Heaven . . . was it?

Mike came in wearing his old Levis and a sweatshirt with cut-off sleeves. He was smiling. The kitchen smelled like Heaven but they knew this roast wasn't plant-based.

"Where's that bottle that needs the cork popped?"

Dinner was a success. The candles were romantic even though twilight was an hour away. The coconut cheesecake was the perfect dessert. They took their flutes into the living room, sat on the sofa holding hands, and watched the sunset turn the buttermilk clouds hues of intense cerise, slowly cooling to soft pink, and finally, a quiet grey.

"Wow . . . that was spectacular. When you had this house built, did you put the glass wall on the west side so you could watch the sunset?"

"Genius, huh!"

"Yes, and incredibly self-effacing about it."

"That's me. Humble, unassuming, and retiring."

Ruby smiled and poured the last of the champagne into his flute.

"Darlin', I have some good news to share, too."

"And you kept quiet while I strutted around and patted myself on the back? Tell me so we can both celebrate."

"I'm pretty excited about this. Abdul came to see me today with an offer of two weeks as a different kind of Angel. It's the metaphysical prize I asked for originally. It wasn't available then, but now it is. I'm going to be the Angel of Death!"

Mike slowly set his glass on the table and lowered his head into his hands. Ruby watched, silent.

"It won't be one bit dangerous darling. I'll have a special phone that will ring when . . . I'm needed. Abdul will show up in his cab and take me to where the uh, situation, is about to happen. I'll sort of, do my thing. Buster will be my assistant. It's just two weeks. Easy Peasy!"

"Why, Ruby?" He looked at her. "Why would you be *excited* about putting people to death? This is sick!"

"It's not like *that*, Mike. I wanted this job because I'll be able to save innocent souls that aren't supposed to die yet. I won't be the Grim Reaper. I'll be a true Angel. I'll have real powers. Then I'll come home and be a plain wife, with no Angel powers, until the next call."

"That scruffy cab driver told you all this? And you believed him? Have you forgotten that our precious child is growing in your womb?"

"Number one, you *know* Abdul is an advanced Angel. His look is his cover. Secondly, you *know* from our Heaven experience, that he's one hundred percent the real deal. And number *three*, our very precious child is a fetus that is one inch long at this stage, and if you don't trust that I will never do ANYTHING to hurt our child, then we need to re-examine our relationship, Michael Harrington!"

He leaned back, rubbed his eyes, and ran his hand through his black curls.

"I suppose you've already made up your mind to do this," he mumbled.

"Well . . . yes. Unless you can show me a valid reason why I shouldn't."

"What if . . . someone pulls a gun and shoots you?"

"Shoots the Angel of Death? I . . . I don't think that can happen, but Mike, what if you approach a man on the street for an interview, and he pulls a gun and shoots you? Does that make your job more dangerous than mine?"

"I should know better than to argue with you," he muttered.

They sat, looking at the darkened scene outside. Ruby took Mike's hand.

"Will you have a territory, or is your jurisdiction worldwide?" he asked.

"I asked that too. Just Denver."

She pulled a small, pink cell phone from her pocket. "This is it, Mike. I start tomorrow."

# Chapter 37

Her pink phone blared a jazzed-up version of taps. Ruby thought how inappropriate it sounded and then realized it was her first summons.

It was midday. Mike was at the television station, taking meetings with the powers that be. Ruby was making herself a sandwich.

"Oh, crap. I'm not exactly dressed . . . how does the Angel of Death dress? Not in rolled-up jeans and a flannel shirt. I should have gotten a manual. Help!"

Her phone blared again, and the front door knocker filled the house with a loud insistent need. Ruby ran and opened the door.

"Afternoon, Miss Ruby." Abdul wore oversized aviator glasses and a colorful Hawaiian shirt.

"Abdul! I need to change clothes! I'm not dressed like an Angel of Death!"

"No time! Let's go. I'll explain on the way."

In a whirl, she was seated in the back of the cab. Buster curled beside her, napping. Ruby watched, as traffic sorted itself out of the cab's way, opening a clear path.

"Good driving, Abdul. Where are we going?"

"A shooting at the Cinna-Bun store in the Mid-Town Mall."

"Oh, dear. When did it happen?"

"It's just about to happen. We'll get there one second later. When your phone chimes, Miss Ruby, you're on metaphysical time."

Questions swirled in Ruby's mind. One second after? Her stomach lurched.

"Buster," she whispered. "What if I get there and pass out, or worse, throw up? I've never seen a person who's been shot. I want to go back to the house. I don't feel well."

"Abdul," she called.

Buster sat up and placed a paw on her leg. She looked into his expressive eyes. She *could* do this.

"Yes, Miss?"

"Uh . . . why are you being so formal? Just talk to me like you would talk to your sister."

"Yes, Miss. I don't have a sister."

At the mall, Ruby and Buster glided past the large fountain into the main entrance, as if they were on roller skates. Ruby had butterflies in her stomach, but Buster exuded confidence for both of them. They glided up the escalator, somehow missing clumps of giggling teens in shorts and tight tees and moms holding their toddlers' hands. Nobody noticed them. At the top, the skates knew which direction to turn. They sailed past the Indian jewelry store and Victoria's Secret. The aroma of cinnamon buns filled the air. Ruby's stomach grumbled, reminding her she hadn't eaten lunch.

Two ear-blasting shots rang out. In no passage of time, Ruby and Buster were at the Cinna-Bun store. The sound waves of the gunshots still reverberated in the high-ceilinged space. A mall security guard stood, his pistol gripped in both hands. A woman dressed in a gold and brown gingham uniform, sprawled on the floor. She looked fresh-faced and young, with two short pigtails tied with yellow ribbons. A lethal-looking handgun lay between the woman and a man curled in a fetal position. He'd been shot in the thigh. Blood pumped out of his femoral artery. He lay in a growing pool of blood.

Ruby kneeled beside the woman, whose eyes were tightly closed, her mouth grimaced in pain. Blood spreading across the top of her pinafore didn't quite obliterate her name embroidered above the pocket. Linnie.

Ruby gently laid a fingertip on her forehead. Linnie opened her eyes.

"Am I going to die?"

Ruby picked up her limp hand.

"You're going to be alright." Her voice sounded like Glenda the Good's. She waved her hand over the woman's body.

The woman's face relaxed.

"Who are you?" Linnie whispered.

"I'm your friendly, neighborhood Angel of Death, dear." A melodic sweep of harp strings accompanied her declaration.

Ruby turned to the injured man. He was past middle age. His head had been messily shaved. She saw a crude tattoo of a clenched fist on his neck. Icy, blue eyes traveled slowly up Ruby's legs, finally reaching her eyes.

"Who the hell are you?" he snarled, his words contorted with pain.

"First, tell me your name," she said. Her voice sounded deep and slow like a record at the wrong speed.

"Daffy Duck. What's yours?"

"Why did you shoot Linnie, Mr. Duck?"

"I didn't. That worthless guard shot her."

Ruby looked for Buster, who was sniffing the corner of a large planter, unmindful of his lie-detecting duties.

"Buster, come!" Buster continued his investigation of the world's most interesting planter, finally choosing a corner to add his signature with a lift of his back leg.

"Don't lie with your last breath, Daffy. Why did you shoot her?"

"Listen to me," he said, his voice thin with pain. "She set off an alarm, ran out with that big-ass purse . . . I grabbed at it . . . she called me a creep, and she . . . "

"So you shot her," Ruby interrupted. "You're not a nice man. I'm going to ask you the most important question of your life. If I let you live, will you promise to change and become a good man?"

He closed his eyes. Chalky-white now, he grunted the words through clenched teeth.

"Fuck you . . . Sweetheart."

She turned away as his eyes rolled up. Buster jumped nimbly into the planter, hunched among the split-leaf philodendrons, and relieved himself.

"My name . . . ," she paused, "is Death."

Ruby turned to a growing group of onlookers. Two suits were talking to the security guard, who had holstered his weapon. Sirens sounded in the distance.

"Security alarm . . . the safe. She . . ." Ruby only heard snatches of his explanation over the din of the thrill-seeking crowd.

"Buster, come!"

She saw Buster wending his way through the copse of legs.

"He just wandered in to buy a bun," the guard said. "He got in her way and she shot him. She pointed the gun at me. I . . . "

Buster growled and ran toward the escalator. Ruby stumbled along behind him.

# Chapter 38

An ambulance pulled up, lights flashing, and siren dying as Ruby and Buster headed for Abdul's yellow taxi.

"Second level," she called to two EMTs as they piled out of the white van, pulled out a gurney, and turned it toward the mall entrance.

"Turn left at the top of the escalator." They didn't seem to hear her.

"Excuse me," Ruby called loudly as the scrubs-clad man and woman barreled toward her. She jumped back, barely missing Buster, who yipped. She watched as they rushed into the mall.

"They can't see you, Miss." Abdul put on his aviators to block out the late afternoon sun.

Ruby and Buster got in and settled themselves into the velour seat.

"The shooting victims could see us. Did the guard know we were there?"

"No, Miss. Only the dying can see you. That's the way it works," he said.

Ruby closed her eyes. Two tears trickled down her cheeks. She stroked Buster's neck under his silky ears.

"How did it go in the mall, Miss?"

She didn't want to talk about her botched decision. She didn't even want to think about it. Her *first* mission. Ruby Louise, the Angel of Death, the savior of good people let the wrong person die and saved the murderer. She put her head on her knees and silently sobbed. One sob escaped, filling the cab.

"Want to talk about it, Miss?" Abdul asked quietly.

Tell her terrible mistake to Abdul? Who else did she have? She didn't know what Mike would say, and she didn't want to find out.

"Abdul, why do I need to look like someone else now if only the dying can see me?"

"A very good reason, Miss. If you saved someone's life, and later, that person saw the other Ruby Louise in the pet supply store, who looked like the Angel, complications could plague you both . . . Miss," he added, belatedly.

"Abdul?"

"Yes, Miss?"

"Oh, never mind. I had a question but it slipped my mind. I guess I'm tired."

"Being the Angel of Death will do that to you, Miss. You've had a big day."

"But I failed, didn't I?" She wondered why she thought he would know. He had stayed in the taxi while she went into the mall.

Ruby closed her eyes. She remembered when her life was simple and calm before she went to that movie and won the Metaphysical Lottery. Mr. Boone . . . cleaning up dog poo . . . coming out of the parakeet cage decorated in bird droppings . . . She didn't want her old life back.

"We're here, Miss."

Ruby opened her eyes.

"Abdul, I'm not good at this job. Can the real Angel of Death take over? I made a terrible mistake today. I saved the wrong person and let a good person die. I'm a—" her voice sank to a whisper, " . . . murderer."

Abdul turned, resting his arm along the top of the seat. His expression was sympathetic.

"No, Miss. The real Angel is on vacation. Can't be reached." He paused. "Do you think Angels can't make a mistake? We both know death isn't always fair. In fact, it seldom is. Do the very best you can."

She climbed out of the taxi. Buster rose with his front feet on the window sill to watch her go. It was the golden hour just before sunset but the softened atmospheric glow was wasted on Ruby.

"Thank you, Abdul."

"And Miss, you actually did it right."

"What did you just say?"

"I said you don't need to thank me. It's my job, Miss."

"Huh. Well, good night."

Ruby closed the door quietly, sat on the sofa, and took off her shoes. She heard the shower running and Mike singing. He sounded happy.

Unable to stop thinking about the deadly mistake she'd made, Ruby re-lived the scene: the pretty Cinna-Bun employee on the floor, blood spreading on her pinafore. It looked like someone had shot Dorothy in the Land of Oz except this Dorothy was a thief and a murderer named Linnie.

Ruby sank to the floor with a whimper. Duchess snuggled under her arm and gave her cheek, salty with tears, a tiny lick.

"I let a man die whose only mistake was to get in Linnie's way, Duchess. He seemed . . . so thuggish! I *suck* at this job. I thought I could . . . I don't know . . . help people."

Duchess licked her chin.

"Cut it out. I know you're trying to cheer me up but your tongue tickles." She sat up. "Are you hungry?" Duchess bounced around, kneeled on her front elbows, butt in the air, and wagged her tail. Ruby walked into the service room and filled their crockery dishes with kibble.

She wandered back into the living room and again sank to the floor, trying to remember something Abdul said in the cab. Did he say I did it right? I was so exhausted . . . he wasn't even there. That bad girl is walking around free, and the poor man . . . Ruby shuddered. What if he was someone's dad? Or a janitor in a school, loved by all the children, and I, the so-called Angel of Death, callously wiped out this paragon of virtue with a wave of my hand?

# Chapter 39

Ruby heard drawers open and close. She didn't want Mike to see her looking devastated after her first day. She hurried into the kitchen, set a large pot of water on the stove, and turned the burner on high.

"Ah, there you are," Mike said. He wrapped his arms around her and kissed her. "I'm spoiled you know," he said. "We've spent all of our days together, and now, you go your way, and I go mine. I miss you."

"I miss being with you too, Mike. I don't even have time to plan a nice meal or order the necessities to pull one off. I'm boiling water for pasta, and I don't even know if we have any."

"Do you like Chinese?" Mike turned off the burner.

"I love Chinese, but I don't want to go out. You don't happen to . . . "

"Of course I do. Pull out a beer for me and something soft for you while I call in an order of Moo Goo Gai Pan and one Moo Shu Pork. We'll share."

Mike found her sitting in the living room staring at the darkened window. No beer and no tea. He sat beside her and picked up her hand.

"Hard first day on the job?"

"N-no." She turned and stared at him. "How did you know?"

"Might have been the tear streaming down your cheek that tipped me off . . . tell me about it, Rube."

"I can't," she whispered.

"Can't or won't? I know you, Ruby. You think I'll say, I *told* you not to take Abdul's job!"

Ruby looked at him. "If I tell you, do you promise not to say that?"

Mike cocked his head. "If I don't promise will you tell me anyway?"

"Absolutely not!"

Mike grinned at her. "Okay. I promise."

"Do you promise not to say anything that still means that?"

Mike raised his hands. "I promise, Ruby. Now tell me about your day."

So she told him about the Cinna-Bun girl in the brown and gold gingham pinafore, and the thuggish man, both sprawled on the mall floor with a gun lying between them, and the mall guard still holding his handgun. "They were both shot, Mike. I chose to think the young woman was the innocent party, and I let the man die."

She paused. "But, what if I was wrong?"

Mike was quiet. She looked hard at him, trying to see what he was thinking.

"How were you supposed to know what had happened, Ruby?"

"I don't know. I guess I thought, as the Angel of Death, I would have special insight. The man wasn't very nice. He told me his name was Daffy Duck . . . he snarled it at me."

Mike took her two hands into his. He looked into her eyes. "Ruby," he said quietly, "you *do* have special insight. You must know that you did the right thing. Don't second guess your instinct. Are you still on call as the Angel of Death?"

"As far as I know. I haven't heard otherwise. Why do you ask?"

"This was your first day on the job. What if this was a test to see if you could handle . . . you *know*, very few strong people could have handled that tough situation. You, Ruby, handled it like a pro. You passed the test! You chose right!"

"I hadn't thought of it that way. Maybe you're right. It's a possibility, isn't it? I learned one important thing, though. Next time, I'll let Buster relieve himself *before* we get to the crisis."

"So he was no help?"

"None, whatsoever. He was in the planter, almost like he was deliberately staying out of the situation."

"Aha! That confirms my theory. You, alone, had to make the hard decision. Doesn't it all add up, Ruby?"

The door knocker sounded. Mike took delivery of the massive order of food. The house filled with mouth-watering aromas.

# Chapter 40

After going on her first call in jeans and a flannel shirt, today, Ruby put on a denim dress and slip-on sandals.

She'd been building an afternoon snack when her phone played taps.

In the cab, Ruby sighed. "Where are we going, Abdul?"

"City Hospital, Miss."

Buster and Ruby entered the main lobby and sailed past the admittance desk, where a woman, wearing round, purple glasses, didn't look up.

"There's an advantage, Buster, of not being visible, but of course, it means we also can't stop and ask directions."

But in an instant, she realized that, somehow, she did know where to go. She shook her head as they stepped confidently into an elevator and stepped out the next time it stopped. At the next corner, they turned right, and three rooms down, stepped through a door. An elderly woman lay in a narrow bed. Sparse, white hair framed her tiny wrinkled face. Her eyes were closed. Arms, barely more than skin and bones, lay on top of the white covers.

Another woman, so immense, Ruby wondered how one chair could hold her, dabbed at her eyes. Hair, the matt-black of a cheap dye job, curled girlishly around her pretty face. Drawn, exaggerated eyebrows competed with her other features, and won. Nothing on her face indicated that she could see, or hear, Ruby and Buster.

After glancing at the chart on the foot of the bed, Ruby approached the bedside and gently took the dying woman's hand.

"Hello, Celia," she said quietly.

Celia opened pale, blue eyes and slowly turned her head. "Oh, you're here. What took you so long?" Her voice was thin, barely above a whisper.

Ruby considered her answer. "I waited until your companion could tell you goodbye."

"She's a vulture."

Ruby leaned in close to hear. Celia's eyes closed. "Get rid of her," she finally whispered. Two tears slid down her temples.

Ruby wondered if the woman across the bed had heard. She was examining her blood-red, acrylic nails.

"I'll try. What's her name?"

There was another long pause.

"Arugula," she whispered. "Her mother named her after a vegetable."

A tiny smile lifted the corners of the dying woman's mouth. "Should have named her Kale," she slowly whispered. "I *like* Arugula."

Ruby considered her options. She realized she had none.

"Rats, Buster. How am I going to get this woman to leave the room?"

Buster tipped his head and then ran around the bed.

"Ouch! Something bit me! Ouch! OUCH! I'm getting out of here. Bye, Aunt Ce . . . OUCH!"

She moved quite nimbly for such a large woman. Buster stood at the door and watched her scurry down the hall, stopping only to rub one ankle and then the other.

Celia's eyes were closed but a peaceful smile graced her face.

"Are you ready to go?" Ruby asked in her soft Angel of Death voice.

"Oh, yes. Hold my hand, dear. Please."

As Ruby slowly swept her free hand over Celia, "Swing Low Sweet Chariot," sung by what sounded like a choir of angels, filled the room. Celia's hand relaxed.

"We did it, Buster. Thanks for your quick thinking."

They were quiet as they rode the elevator down. She knew Buster was thinking about dinner, a satisfying drink of water, and a long night's sleep on his own soft bed, wherever that was.

It was dark when Ruby and Buster came out of the hospital entrance. A fingernail-clipping moon had risen. Abdul stood at the open back door of the cab while Buster found an arborvitae to anoint.

Leaning back on the seat as they traveled home, Buster curled up on her lap, deep in dreamland.

"How was your day?" she asked Abdul.

"Eventful, Miss Ruby. How was yours?"

Eventful? Ruby remembered stepping back out of the hospital entrance and being surprised that her driver, and the cab she thought of as his home, were gone. She almost asked Abdul where he'd gone, but reconsidered.

"We let a sweet, ancient lady go. It was nice. Her passing was accompanied by an angelic choir. I didn't know I could do that." She stroked Buster's furry, brown neck.

The cab pulled into the driveway and stopped. Ruby climbed out and walked slowly up the steps.

The door flew open. Mike picked up Ruby and kissed her. "I got it, Rube! I'm now Michael Harrington, Man on the Street!" He carried her into the house and after a twirl, set her down.

"You're married to a certified interviewer. This is going to be so fun."

"I'm so happy for you. Let's pour something, and celebrate. Make mine a double."

"Oh, right. Your second day. Was it tough? Want to tell me about it?"

"No. But I'll tell you . . . it was sweet and gratifying. Now. How about that drink?"

"I've done a little research, Rube. Pregnancy has a tendency to be emotionally challenging. It might be too hard for you."

"Mike, if I come home a crying wreck every night, I'll consider resigning. Now, let's celebrate your new position. I can hardly wait to see your first television interview. You'll be great!"

# Chapter 41

Ruby showered and changed into lounge pants and a cashmere sweater. She slid into her bunny slippers.

Mike cooked hamburgers while Ruby sat at the kitchen bar sipping her mocktail: ginger beer and tonic with a splash of grenadine.

"Our home is a metaphysical-free zone, Mike."

"Really? In what way, specifically?"

"Well, when I go on call only the dying can see me. To the living, I'm not there and neither is Buster."

Mike was slicing a tomato. He put the knife down. "You're *invisible?*"

"I am. I almost got knocked down by an EMT before Abdul told me."

Mike's eyes got big. "Can you see yourself?"

"Of course, and before you ask, I look like myself. There's no time to change clothes when I hear the summons. I've gone out in my jeans. Nobody dying seemed to care."

"What if you get a summons while you're in the shower?"

"Ooo, that would be bad . . . wrapped in a towel, with dripping hair. I should leave a step-in dress on the bed so I can dress on the way to the door."

Mike's eyebrows shot up. "No underwear?"

"No time. The dying won't care. It worked in Heaven. You eventually liked it."

"Yeah. It did work in Heaven. Now, every morning when I get dressed, I think about no underwear. Why *do* we wear it?"

Ruby laughed. "Convention, I guess."

"Oops!" Mike said, tiring of the underwear subject. "Don't want to overcook the burgers. Fries are in the oven, crisping up."

He plated the meal and added a dollop of his secret sauce, which was simply horse radish and catsup. He pulled out Ruby's chair for her and with a flair, put her cloth napkin in her lap. He sat, and they smiled at each other.

"This is nice, Mike. Thank you for cooking dinner tonight. I love hamburgers."

With the dishwasher running, they sat together on the sofa with cups of coffee and admired the evening sky. Duke and Duchess crashed out at their feet.

"Um, at the risk of sounding crude," Mike murmured into Ruby's hair, "think we could risk a little lovin' without that stupid pink gadget spoiling our fun?"

"Won't know until we try."

"You could stuff it under the couch cushion."

"Can't do that, Sweetheart. I'm committed to complete integri—" At that point, the stupid pink gadget in question blared.

"Sorry, Darlin'! We'll play catch-up when I get back. Remember, it's just for two weeks." She ran to the door, which Abdul was pounding on.

Mike groaned.

# Chapter 42

"Abdul, would you answer some questions for me?" Ruby asked as he drove out of the circle driveway and entered the street.

"Certainly, Miss Ruby. What would you like to know?"

There was so much she wondered about him. Despite his unkempt appearance, when she looked into his hazel eyes, she saw a caring Angel who undeniably knew things she hadn't dreamed of.

"Abdul, how long have you had this job, and what did you do before?" she asked.

"Sixteen years and before, I was a New York City cabbie."

"Huh. Did you submit a resume to the professor?"

"No ..."

The question hung in the air between them.

"Miss Ruby, remember when you arrived at the mall shooting one second before the shots rang out?"

"Oh, I wish you hadn't reminded me of that call. I may have made a terrible mistake, and it will haunt me forever."

"Actually, you did well. The man was the perpetrator. He forced the young woman to rob the safe for him. He put the gun in her hand to shoot the guard. She shot him instead. You saved her and let the criminal die."

Ruby stared at him. "You knew. Why didn't you tell me?"

"I did," he said quietly. "In the cab on the way back to your home. Remember? That's all I can tell you, but Miss Ruby, I've given you the answer to your question."

She saw a small smile on his face.

"Another thing, Abdul. Why aren't there any gruesome deaths in this city? No mashed people in cars, no suicide hangings, no bloody bathtub murders, no slasher victims, or burned-up people in fires. What's going on?"

"Not your department," he said.

She wondered what her department was called. Department of Gentle Deaths? Maybe Department of Deaths for Dummies. D.O.D.D. She sighed. At least day one had turned out to be good. Mike was right. She smiled.

Ruby heard sirens. Abdul pulled into a parking space.

"I'll wait here," he said.

Ruby and Buster climbed out. Cars were backed up for a block. Drivers honked their horns. She heard a few curses hurled out of windows.

"Come on, Buster. Let's see what happened." They ran to the bottleneck and saw a car stalled diagonally in the street. The engine was running, but the car didn't appear to have hit anything. The driver was slumped against the steering wheel.

"Help me get him out of the car," she called to an onlooker. He couldn't see or hear her. She opened the car door and pulled on the man. His large body came easily. Surprised, she put her arms under his shoulders and legs. He was portly, but it felt like he weighed no more than a small child. As she gently laid him on the street, his hairpiece came off his head.

"Oh crap, Buster! It's Mr. Boone, and he's lost his toupee!"

Her former Pet City boss gurgled, turned red, and stopped breathing. Ruby waved her arm in a circle over his prone body.

A life-giving force traveled from her fingertips to the man's chest with an audible snap.

The ambulance and fire truck pulled up, their sirens abruptly silenced, but garish red and blue shafts of color flashed onto the scene.

Ruby turned off the engine.

Mr. Boone opened his eyes and looked around. "What happened?" he asked.

Two men in blue scrubs ran to his side with a stretcher.

"I'll tell you what happened," an onlooker said. "A few seconds ago, you were out cold, slumped on your steering wheel. Then, your door opened, and you just leaned out, dead to the world, and *floated* down to the street! I couldn't believe my eyes. Damnedest thing I ever saw. You turned an awful color, and then you came *to*! Unbelievable! Wait 'til I tell my wife!" He walked away muttering to himself and waving his hands.

"We're going to take you to the hospital, Mister. You've had a dangerous blackout."

Mr. Boone sat up. "No need. I'm perfectly alright." He picked up his toupee, clapped it onto his head, rolled to his knees, and stood. He brushed off his pants, climbed into his car, started it, and drove away.

Drivers, impatient to get wherever bore down on her. She yelped and jumped fifteen feet to the curb. Shaking, she sank to the grass.

"Buster, did you see that?"

He tipped his head like, so?

He dog-pranced back to the parked cab. As Ruby climbed in, she pictured Mr. Boone at a fancy social function when he discovered that his toupee sat sideways on his head.

Ruby walked into the house with a smile.

"Easy one?" Mike asked.

"Well, yes. Remember when we went to the Pet City to buy dog food? Mr. Boone, my former—"

"Let's don't talk shop, Rube," Mike interrupted. "If you remember, we were—"

"Oh, I remember," she cut him off. "Before I was summoned, we were talking about some serious bedroom time. I haven't forgotten."

"Or, wherever," Mike said, as he wiggled his eyebrows at her.

But she was already walking down the hall, pulling off her sweater.

"Bedroom, Lover. Dog audiences put me off."

Duke and Duchess looked at each other.

# Chapter 43

"I'm starving, dogs. Let's eat something before that cursed phone rings."

After plopping two bacon slices into a hot skillet, Ruby picked up their dishes. "Kibbles or hamburger?"

Seeing their looks, she broke a raw patty in two and added a handful of kibble into each dish. When she'd eaten half of her BLT, the phone pealed taps.

*I knew it! This is turning into a full-time job.*

"Where to, Abdul?"

"One of the city's oldest neighborhoods. Nice old homes and quiet streets."

They drove down a shady avenue. Manicured lawns and walks bordered by banks of flowering plants, led to Victorian-style homes.

"This is it." He stopped in front of a majestic sky-blue house. It had a turret, two lead-glass bay windows, and a porticoed porch.

"Wow," she said under her breath. Buster and Ruby walked up the worn brick path. White wrought-iron hand rails led up steps to the porch. She pressed the brass doorbell. Sonorous chimes played eight full notes.

A tall, dignified man dressed like an old-timey butler opened the door. He peered out, and not seeing anybody, stepped onto the porch and looked behind the door.

Ruby and Buster slipped inside.

"I'm not feeling any pull, Buster."

They didn't find anyone in the sitting room. It was furnished with a peacock-style velvet settee, side tables with matching bronze lamps, and Tiffany, dragonfly shades. A worn Persian rug covered the dark, hardwood floor. They walked quickly through the formal dining room into the kitchen. A swarthy, sea-faring-looking man wearing a white tee with rolled-up sleeves and a blood-spattered white apron sat at a pine work table, massacring a large piece of beef with a cleaver.

Ruby noted a back door and two other doors which might lead to a pantry and a cellar.

"Upstairs," said Buster.

At the landing, they hurried through a slightly open door. Inside, sat a huge, four-poster bed. A large mahogany armoire stood against the wall. Ruby slowly opened the door just enough to see vintage gowns hanging on satin hangers. The unmistakable odor of mothballs brought tears to her eyes. She closed the door.

Buster was already trotting down the hall.

"No buzz yet," Ruby mumbled.

Three of the doors down the hall led to empty bedrooms. Opening a fourth door, Ruby found a spacious bathroom. A deep, cast-iron bathtub stood on clawed feet across from a clunky pedestal basin. A commode sat on a platform, like a throne. The tank, suspended high on the wall, had a brass chain with a worn wooden handle.

"Nobody dying here, Buster." Around a corner, a short staircase led upward.

"It's the attic. You stay here. I'll take a peek."

Ruby opened the door to a dormer room. On a narrow bed, a young woman wearing a black polyester dress and a white

214

pinafore apron lay on her back, sleeping. Sensible shoes sat on the floor.

Ruby wondered if she'd stepped into a time warp.

"We've looked everywhere but the two doors in the kitchen," she told Buster. "If we don't find anything there, it's a false alarm."

They hurried down the staircase and retraced their steps into the kitchen. The cook still sitting at the table, his back to them, now chopped vegetables. On the stove, which looked to be the same vintage as the home, a large pot sent up meaty steam.

Ruby peeked in one of the doors. She saw shelves of canisters labeled flour, sugar, and other staples.

She opened the second door, slowly, hoping it wouldn't squeak. Stairs led down, no light switch on the wall. Groping ahead, she felt a string and pulled it. Buster stayed close on Ruby's heels. A small bulb in the middle of the room gave off enough light for them to carefully descend after quietly closing the door. She harbored an aversion to dank, dim places.

Buster went to the middle of the room and stood sniffing. A faint buzz told Ruby she'd finally found the dying person. Wishing she had a flashlight, she found herself being drawn to a huge cast-iron furnace on the back wall. With a loud clunk, she threw the bolt. The thick metal door, large enough to accommodate a coal chute, swung open with a hideous screech.

*Nothing to be done if the cook comes to investigate.*

They waited.

# Chapter 44

The cook stood in the doorway, his legs spread in a combat-ready stance, the cleaver clutched in his hand. His eyes swept the room and stopped at the open furnace door.

"Huh," he grunted, and came down the stairs slowly, eyes darting around the room. He leaped off the bottom step and jumped toward the space under the staircase, cleaver poised. Then he walked straight to the furnace and still scanning the room, slammed the door closed with another ear-jarring screech.

Ruby's heart sank. Whoever was in there, was going to have a wait while she tried to open the door without making a noise.

Satisfied there were no intruders, the cook stomped up the stairs and pulled the light string, plunging the cellar into inky darkness.

Not even a thin line shone under the kitchen door. Ruby crawled slowly up the filthy steps, clinging to the wall. "I hate this job," she muttered. When she banged her head on the kitchen door, she froze. *If the cook opens the door, pulls the string, and comes down, I'll be trampled, and we'll both end up at the bottom of the stairs with the cleaver sunk into one of us, probably me.*

She counted to twenty, stood, and pulled the string. Buster waited beside the furnace. "Hurry," he growled.

"I'm coming. Got any ideas for opening the furnace?"

"Oil?"

Looking at the contents of the one shelf, she saw cans of paint and voila! Motor oil. *Nothing to open the can with.* "My kingdom for a church-key." *Can't wait any longer.*

Ruby turned the handle, and holding her breath, slowly, inch by inch, opened the door. With a two-inch gap, the faint light shone on the soles of two large cowboy boots, pointy toes up. When she could get her arm in, she circled it over the man and felt a faint snap, signaling her life force had arrested his death. Giving silent thanks, and aware that her hand had been directly over his crotch, she wondered if he would come out with a raging erection. "*Bad* girl," she whispered, wiping the smile off her face.

Now that the man inside the furnace was no longer dying, he couldn't see *or* hear her. And the door still wasn't open wide enough to get him out.

"Buster, I need to get Abdul. You stay here and watch him."

Ruby climbed the stairs and quietly opened the door to the kitchen. The cook sat with his back to the cellar door, his feet up on another chair. He lit a cigar, took a puff, and blew smoke rings in the air. On the table sat a half-drank bottle of Coors.

She closed the door but didn't latch it and scrambled through the dining room, the sitting room, and out the front door. Ruby ran down the walk and tapped on the cab window. Abdul opened the door.

"Abdul, someone tried to murder a man in the house. They put him in the furnace. I need you to help."

"But," he started to protest.

"There's an outside door. Hurry!"

She handed him a key she'd found on a hook beside the kitchen entrance.

They ran to the side of the house where slanted cellar doors were latched with a hasp and a padlock. Abdul fitted the key in, and they pulled the doors open.

Buster stood watch as daylight flooded the dingy room. "Just in time," he said. "He's moving around in there."

"Careful. Don't open the furnace door any wider. It screeches."

Abdul reached into his pocket and brought out a tube of lip moisturizer. He squirted it on the hinges and pulled the door open, silently. "Petroleum," he whispered.

Together, they reached in and pulled out the dazed, sooty man.

"Can you stand?" Abdul whispered. "I'm going to get you out of the house." He put his finger to his lips in a 'be quiet' gesture.

The African American man had green eyes and long eyelashes that curled up. He looked to be in his mid-twenties, as tall as Abdul, but boyishly slender. Blood seeped from his back. He wasn't totally aware yet.

Ruby and Abdul hooked their shoulders under each of his arms and walked him to the open cellar doors. The three-foot drop into the room posed a problem until Abdul twirled his finger. They turned him around, backed the man up to the ledge, and each taking hold under a thigh, hoisted him out.

Abdul pointed to himself, to the young man, and to the cab.

"Got it. See what information you can get from him. Buster and I are going back in. We might be able to sort out the would-be murderer."

Up the cellar stairs, Ruby opened the door just enough to peek into the kitchen. The cook, still enjoying his break, listened to a small radio. She pulled the light string, they stepped into the kitchen, and quietly closed the door.

"He's in the clear Buster, because when he came into the cellar, he didn't even look in the furnace. We can check him off our list of suspects."

"Maybe," Buster growled. "But I don't like the looks of his bloody apron."

"Good point. I'll put a question mark beside his name."

"Let's find the butler. In mystery novels, the butler always does it."

She opened the front door, rang the doorbell, and quickly stepped back in. The butler came out of a room down the hall, closed his door, and pulled on his morning coat. Ruby and Buster stepped into his room. "What are we looking for?" Buster asked.

"A knife. Those were stab wounds."

The room was a sitting room, bath, and bedroom. Ruby pulled open a dresser drawer. Old-fashioned button-up undershorts ironed and stacked. Another drawer held starched white shirts, folded, and stacked. Among black socks in a third drawer, she saw a metallic glint. As she reached for it, the butler came in. He saw the open drawer, a frown on his face. Ruby jumped out of the way and knocked her elbow into a lamp on the dresser.

He froze. His eyes moved back and forth. "Maddie, is that you?" He turned, looking for the mysterious Maddie. He reached into the sock drawer, pulled out a tiny handgun, ejected the clip, checked that it was still loaded, and shoved it back under the black socks.

They watched but could see there was no knife. He carefully hung his morning coat in the closet. Then he sat in the easy chair by the window and picked up the book he'd left open, *The Hounds of Baskerville*. Ruby smiled and motioned to Buster.

When the butler's eyes were on the page, they slipped out of the room.

"We can cross him off the suspect list."

"Unless he buried the knife in the flower bed," Buster said.

"Okay, Watson. I'll put a question mark beside his name, too."

They went up the elegant curved staircase, carpeted with a worn Turkish runner. On the wall, framed portraits of stern-faced ancestors seemed to follow them with cold eyes. Ruby shivered. "Buster, was this staircase like this when we went up before?"

"I don't remember," Buster growled.

They stepped into the ruffley room. The armoire, empty now, no longer smelled like moth balls.

"Okay, one more suspect. The proverbial upstairs maid. If she's gone, I'm turning in my magnifying glass."

They opened each of the three doors down the hall. All were unoccupied, exactly as before. Around the corner, they climbed the stairs leading to the attic room.

"Stay close to me, Buster. I'm getting creeped out."

Ruby quietly opened the door. The woman, dressed in the same black polyester dress and white pinafore apron, still lay on the bed, but she had turned toward the wall.

"I'm going to see if she's alive." Just as Ruby leaned over her, the woman snorted, opened her eyes, looked at her watch, and sat up. She hurriedly thrust stockinged feet into her shoes. She had green eyes and brown, curly hair pulled into a ponytail. She looked vaguely familiar. The woman stood, looked around, patted her apron pockets, and left the room. They followed her down the stairs and into the dining room.

From a large sideboard, she took out an ivory tablecloth and smoothed it onto the table. At one end, she placed a dinner plate, a bread plate, a linen napkin, and silverware. From another door of the dark cabinet, she brought out a stemmed wine glass and a matching water goblet. A large, silver candelabra completed the setting.

Ruby wondered who would be dining alone at this table. Would it be the man in the furnace? He didn't look like the type that would dress for dinner.

"If the maid set this up for our victim, she's off the suspect list."

"Unless she's a very *clever* murderer," he answered.

"So we have three suspects or none. We need to see what Abdul found out from the furnace man."

# Chapter 45

"Hey, Buddy," Abdul said softly. "You had a close call."

The young man sat slumped in the front seat. He was slim with high cheekbones and a lantern jaw. He turned and looked at Abdul. His hand scrabbled for the door handle.

"Wait! Don't be afraid of me. I pulled you out of the furnace. You're safe now."

"Am I dead?"

"Your back is bloody and covered in furnace soot." Abdul twisted the cap off a bottle of water. "Here. Drink this. No bottled water in the afterlife. You're very much alive."

The tawny man hesitantly reached for the bottle and drank, keeping his eyes on Abdul. When it was empty he handed it back.

"My name's Abdul. What's yours?"

"Thomas," he said shakily. "Thomas Cody."

Ruby and Buster hurried to the cab. They quietly climbed into the back seat. Abdul backed down the street so they weren't parked in front of the Victorian.

"What have you found out?" she asked.

"So Thomas," Abdul said. "Someone in that house tried to kill you. I'm going to do some sleuthing. Do you feel okay about telling me your story?"

"I guess I need some help. Stuff's happening too fast . . . not all of it . . . I live in Wyoming. I got a call from an attorney two weeks ago that my grandmother was on her deathbed and wanted to see me. See, I grew up in foster homes so I didn't know I even *had* a grandmother. God, I'm hungry!"

Ruby passed the bag of corn chips and one of the protein bars stashed in her arm-rest to Abdul. He handed them to Thomas.

Thomas tore the bag open and tipped the chips into his mouth.

"He sent me a plane ticket to Denver, picked me up at the airport, and brought me here," Thomas said, still chewing. "The butler, can you imagine, a butler? He told me my grandmother's name was Madeline. He took me up to the old lady's room and pulled a chair to the bedside. She told him he could leave us. I sat looking at her in the big ol' frilly bed. She laid there, looking at me."

He paused and looked out the window.

"What happened next?" Abdul prompted.

"So bizarre. I keep thinking I'll wake up."

"What did she say?"

"She said her daughter, Rose, that would be my mother, got pregnant with me on the wrong side of the sheet. That's how she put it. When I was born, it came out that she had *dallied,* her word, with a black man. My mother, Grandmother told me, was beautiful. After she came back from where they sent her off to, she was courted by an upstanding gentleman and became engaged."

"So you were put up for adoption?"

"I guess biracial babies weren't in high demand twenty-three years ago. I was shuttled around foster homes until I was of age."

"And then," Abdul prompted.

"She told me I had Rose's eyes. Guess that's where I got this lighter skin, too.

"She asked me to hold her hand and told me my mother and her husband died in a plane crash on their fifth anniversary. They were flying to the Cayman Islands to celebrate. Their daughter, that would be my half-sister, was three. Grandmother told me she regretted that she was seventy, too old to raise a toddler. She lost track of her."

He turned and looked at Abdul. "And then while I held her hand, my grandmother died. She smiled at me . . . and died."

"I'm sorry," Abdul murmured.

Thomas sat, staring at nothing. "Yeah. I'd have liked . . . so anyhow, I started packing to leave, but the attorney showed up, sayin' I should stay for the funeral and the reading of the will. The day after Grandmother was laid to rest, Mr. Banner, that's the attorney's name, came to the house and asked the cook, the butler, the maid, and me to come to the sitting room. Straight out of a corny movie."

"Did you inherit?"

"I still can't believe it, Mr. Abdul. Last week I worked on a horse ranch in Wyoming. It wasn't too hard. The people treated me right. I liked the horses. Arabians. All I owned were my Wranglers, two hats, work shirts, a pair of work boots, and a pair of dress-up boots."

"And now?"

"I'm rich." There was a long pause. "She gave the butler, James is his name, a hundred thousand dollars, and an annuity. He didn't even blink. She gave me this house, some other property in Denver, and seven-and-a-half million dollars! I almost fainted. Million!" He looked into Abdul's eyes. "I can't even . . . "

"Ask what she gave the maid and the cook," Ruby said.

225

The young man shook his head and gazed into his long-fingered, calloused hands lying in his lap.

"What did the maid and cook inherit?" Abdul asked.

Thomas came back from where his mind had wandered. "Mr. Banner asked them to follow him into the dining room. He said something so quiet, I couldn't hear, but the maid screamed."

"Good scream or bad scream?"

"Bad scream. Like when the cat's tail gets rocked on. They stayed in there and talked a few more minutes. Mr. Banner came back out, but I didn't see the others. I signed papers and he left."

"Did he leave you a copy of the will?"

"He gave me a bunch of papers but I'd just started to look at them."

"Thomas shouldn't go back into the house," Ruby said. "He could stay in a hotel downtown. When it's dark, I think the murderer will fire up the furnace. I'll stay here and see who goes down to the cellar."

"Thomas," Abdul said, "Do you have any idea who stabbed you? Where were you when it happened?"

"I was sitting at the desk in the bedroom. The one next to Grandmother's room. I was trying to make sense of the papers Mr. Banner gave me. I didn't hear a thing. The next time I opened my eyes, I was in that furnace."

"Maybe you should disappear for a while, for your own safety."

"But if I'm gone, who's there to catch him? Or her. Maybe all three of them."

"After I drop you off, I'll come back with a motion sensor camera. I still have the key to the outside cellar doors."

"Good plan," Thomas said. "Can I sneak in and get some clean clothes first?"

"Too risky. The concierge at the hotel can get you what you need. Do you have a credit card?"

"Hell, yes. And now, I'm a *rich* Wyoming ranch hand."

Abdul started the motor.

"Good idea about the camera," Ruby said. She and Buster slipped out of the car. "We'll need visual proof." She gave him a thumbs-up as he pulled away.

"I'm not keen on sitting in the creepy cellar until it's necessary, Buster. We might learn something by spying on the maid and the cook. And I want to look at the papers the attorney left with Thomas."

After ringing the doorbell Ruby and Buster slipped in as the butler stepped out. "Maddy, Darling, is that you?" he said quietly.

In the dining room, the place setting sat untouched. The maid and the cook played gin rummy on the pine table in the kitchen. He was still in his blood-spattered clothes. A pot of spaghetti cooled on the stove, the tomato-sauce aroma filling the kitchen. A salad and a crusty bagatelle sat on the counter.

"Did you knock on his door?" the cook asked while he shuffled the cards.

"I told you, Dan, he's not here." She took the band from her ponytail, ran her fingers through her brown, curly hair, and put the band on her wrist.

"You should wear it like that, all fluffy and loose," Dan said. "You're kinda pretty with those green eyes."

She gave him a withering look.

"I can't believe he's your brother."

"Half-brother!" she snapped. "I didn't even know he existed. The hick shows up and wins the lottery. I . . . "

"You what, Jackie? Why are you whining? And why did you take this job? According to you, your auntie pays all your bills. You're not poor like me."

"None of your business. I don't want to play cards. You win. I lose, as usual." She huffed out of the swinging door.

Ruby and Buster followed her up the stairs. They watched as she pulled a small suitcase off the shelf of the closet. Jackie stripped out of the uniform she wore. She untied the lace-up shoes and jerked them and the white socks off. Rolling the clothes and the shoes into a bundle, she hurled it out of the open window. She put on a grey pencil skirt and a white linen blouse, fished a pair of grey, kitten-heel sandals from under the bed, and put them on. She emptied a drawer of her underwear into the case, slammed it closed, looked around the room, and left.

In the dining room, Ruby watched her bang the suitcase onto the table, open it, and hurl in the silverware from the place setting. From a drawer in the sideboard, she threw in the rest of the set, a handful at a time.

"What's going on?" the cook yelled, charging through the swinging door from the kitchen, his unibrow raised in disbelief.

"He's rich! He can buy gold forks or eat with his fingers for all I care. I need to get more than minimum wage for six weeks of this stupid, demeaning farce."

"But the lawyer . . . " His eyes shifted around, making sure nobody was in hearing distance.

She interrupted him. "Yeah, *you* can trust that sleaze if you want. I'll be at my aunt's."

Jackie closed the lid, grabbed the handle, and tugged. The case wouldn't move.

"Shit! It's too heavy. Take it out to the curb for me. I called a cab."

"You didn't say the magic word, Jackie. Do your own dirty work. I still need this job." He turned and went into the kitchen without a backward glance.

"Thanks, Sir Galahad." She pulled the suitcase to the edge of the table, taking the tablecloth with it. The dishes crashed into each other, and to the floor, shattering into hundreds of shards. Buster and Ruby jumped back. "Boo-fucking-hoo," she said and pulled the heavy case off the edge. It plunged to the floor, barely missing her foot. The cheap, tweedy case broke open spilling lacy bikini panties, Victoria's Secret bras, and the entire twelve-place setting of ornate silverware onto the hardwood floor.

"Mademoiselle, what do you think you're doing?" the butler boomed. He was in his shirt-sleeves. The handgun Ruby had seen in his drawer, was pointed at the small woman.

She screamed, jumped over the mess on the floor, grabbed the silver candelabra, lying on its side on the table, and ran for the door.

"Watch this, Buster."

Ruby snatched the candelabra out of Jackie's grasp and tossed it into the air. They watched, wide-eyed, and open-mouthed as it tumbled end-over-end in the high-ceilinged room. She caught the candlestick and set it neatly on the table.

"I was a twirler in high school," she announced to Buster.

"Fuck!" Jackie closed her mouth and considered lunging for the candelabra.

"Go!" the butler roared. He waved the gun at her.

She ran out of the house to a cab pulling to the curb. She climbed into the back seat.

"You'll need to wait a couple of minutes, Miss, while I deliver a package," Abdul told her.

# Chapter 46

Abdul walked around the side of the house, while Ruby and Buster slipped quietly through the kitchen to the cellar door. Dan, the cook, ladled spaghetti into a container at the stove. The radio on the table was playing "The Pretender" by Jackson Browne.

Ruby closed the door softly and pulled the string, dimly illuminating the cellar. Abdul opened the slanted doors from the outside, letting the late afternoon light in, and dropped lightly in. They looked for a place to mount the motion-activated camera that would clearly show the murderer's face.

"I've got it, Abdul," Ruby said. "See those boxes piled against the wall? Let's pile them in the corner here and put the camera on top so the perpetrator's face is in plain view. The camera will look like part of the junk. They'll probably only have a flashlight."

They quickly moved the boxes, piled on some old clothing, and arranged the camera.

Ruby pulled the light string and lifted a protesting Buster out of the side door into the yard. She and Abdul sat on the ledge and crawled out. They walked to the cab, thinking Jackie would be waiting there, but she wasn't.

"I guess she called another cab," Abdul said.

"Or sneaked back into the house."

They were quiet on the ride back to the house Ruby had begun to think of as her home. In seven days, her Angel of Death term would be over, and she and Mike would get married. They'd already gotten the marriage license.

"Abdul, I think you should deliver the cellar door key to Thomas. Let him take over sleuthing his would-be killer. You and I have other fish to fry. Do you agree?"

They pulled into the circle driveway. Abdul put the cab in park and turned to Ruby.

"I became sidetracked by the mystery. You are correct. I will take him the key and tell him where the camera is located."

"He can't let you know who it was . . . can he, Abdul?"

"No, and he can't let you know either, Miss Ruby."

"Maybe we'll see it on the evening news," Ruby said.

Mike greeted Ruby with a big smile and a kiss.

"Come with me to the kitchen, my dear, and I'll ply you with . . . do you like Pina Coladas?"

"Will we get caught in the rain?" she answered, going along with the theme.

"We can chance it on the back deck. The dogs want to go out. I'll make the drinks. Change to your comfy duds and meet me there. Take your time."

Ruby gladly shed the clothes she'd crawled up the cellar steps in and stepped into the shower. She wrapped her wet hair in a towel and climbed into jeans and a purple sweatshirt. She joined Mike on the deck barefoot, with a smile on her face. Her drink had a paper umbrella stuck into a slice of lime.

"Where's your umbrella?"

"Pregnant ladies get umbrellas instead of alcohol."

Ruby pulled the umbrella out of the lime and stuck it into the towel on her head.

"Tell me about your day, Mr. Anchorman, and I'll tell you about mine."

"You tell me yours. You'll see mine on the six o'clock news in exactly . . . " he checked his watch, "one hour."

"You might want to alert your networks about this story, Mike. It's definitely newsworthy."

She told him about finding the Wyoming cowboy in the Victorian mansion's cellar furnace with mortal knife wounds in his back. "He's an African American. He grew up in foster homes, never knowing his heritage until a lawyer called with the information of his white grandmother's impending death."

"You saved him?" Mike asked,

"Of course, Mike. That's my job. But Abdul helped me get him out of the furnace without alerting the residents of the house, one of whom is probably the murderer."

She told Mike about Thomas's grandmother dying while they laid eyes on each other for the first time, Thomas's massive inheritance, and the faithful butler who kept expecting to be contacted by Maddy-Dear. There was the cook and the upstairs maid, Jackie, Thomas's half-sister who'd only gone to work there to cash in on her grandmother's will but was left out, completely.

"Cripes!" Mike exclaimed. "It sounds like an Agatha Christie murder mystery."

"It does! Abdul took Thomas to a Hilton Hotel downtown, but as far as the murderer knows, he's still in the furnace, dead. So Abdul bought a motion detection camera. We placed it in the cellar so it will take a photo of the killer's face when he, or she, sneaks down to set fire to Thomas's remains."

"My God, Ruby! Please tell me you're through with that can of worms! You can't be involved with murderers! You're pregnant!"

"Relax, Michael. Abdul took the cellar door key to Thomas so he can retrieve the camera and nail the murderer. I'm out of it. I only told you so you could scoop the other networks with this story."

Mike sat, looking at Ruby.

"What?" she said.

"I need to call . . . but, what should I say when they ask how I know about this?"

"Uh, could you say you were in the Hilton having a beer and struck up a conversation with a cowboy named Thomas Cody who told you about his day?"

# Chapter 47

"Hmm. Not good way to get a news story, Ruby, but it's worthy of looking into. Thomas is staying at the Hilton downtown?"

"That's where Abdul took him."

"I need to think about it, but right now, I'm hungry. Aren't you? When did you eat last?"

"I had half of a BLT mid-morning. I'm starving! Is there anything in the fridge that we can cook? I'm sorry, Mike. I'm not being much of a homemaker these days."

"You sit and sip your Pina Colada. I'm going to call for a pizza with everything. Do you like anchovies?"

"Love them!"

"Then you can have mine."

The next morning, Ruby lolled in bed, watching Mike get dressed. As the evening news anchor, his day didn't start until the afternoon, so he was pulling on jeans and a long-sleeve tee.

She yawned. "I wish I could call the wizard and request a personal day. This job is like work."

"Are you sorry you chose to be Death?" Mike asked.

"Not a bit. Of course, I had no idea what I was getting myself into."

She put her pillow against the headboard and sat back. "When do you start your Man on the Street interviews? Oh! We forgot to watch your newscast last night!"

"We did, but your murder mystery took over my mind. I think I'll go talk to Thomas and see if he would be up for a news interview by a professional."

"Mike, I've been thinking. You can't reference me as your source of information. If he goes to the police with the attempted murder story, and you somehow know about it, you might be implicated."

"So no scoop?"

"I'm just saying that you can't have prior information as far as Thomas is concerned because . . . "

"Of the Angel of Death thing."

"Right."

"So Ruby, Abdul took him downtown to the hotel, right?"

"That's right! Thomas doesn't know about me but he knows about Abdul! He knows Abdul put a camera in the cellar. Mike, if you can find Thomas at the Hilton, tell him that Abdul told you about the attempted murder, and he asked if you could help him identify the murderer. Does that make sense?"

Mike looked at her. "Abdul can't do it?"

"No! We've already signed off. My pink phone might ring any minute, and Abdul will be at the door to take me to the next incident. That's his first priority. *We* can't help Thomas, but *you* can. He doesn't know this city. He probably couldn't tell a cabbie the address to take him to the Victorian. He's a Wyoming cowboy, Mike. He needs help."

"Think he's still at the Hilton?"

"He's probably eating breakfast and wondering how to find his way back to the house he inherited. You won't be able to miss him. He's wearing cowboy boots. And he's tawny. Go, Mike!"

"It would be nice if I knew the address of the house, Ruby."

"Oh. Abdul drove me there so . . . you know the street that those Victorian houses are on? It's sky blue and has a turret. Thomas will be able to pick it out . . . I hope."

Mike shook his head, picked up his wallet and keys, and headed for the garage.

He drove to the Hilton, cruised the parking lot, and found a space on the far perimeter. He'd eaten breakfast at the restaurant with his colleagues before, so he headed straight to it. The smell of bacon reminded Mike that he hadn't eaten this morning. His stomach growled. The large room was typically laid out with booths along the walls and tables and chairs in the middle.

A woman approached him holding menus the size of a chess board.

"I'm joining a diner. Maybe you could help me find him. He's a young African American cowboy."

She broke into a smile. "Follow me," she said and led Mike to a booth on the far side of the room.

"Thomas, here's the friend you're waiting for."

Thomas looked up from the menu. "You're not Abdul."

"Thomas, Abdul couldn't come, but he asked me to fill in for him. I'm here to help. May I sit down?"

Thomas gestured to the settee across the booth.

Before sitting, Mike offered his right hand. "Mike Harrington," he said with a friendly smile.

"Thomas Cody." He shook Mike's hand. "You said Abdul couldn't come but he asked you to help me?"

"He told me about your close call. But he's a cab driver, he had to work today. I'm an anchor on KMGH Channel 7 here in Denver, but I'm not here to put your story on the news. I'm here to take you to the house you inherited and see if your murderer is on that camera. Okay?"

"You would do that for me?"

"Someone who knows you came into a huge amount of money and would benefit from your death, needs to be behind bars. If that person visited the furnace last night and found you gone, you're in danger. You need to be proactive. Do you agree?"

"Well, yeah. But I'm hungry. Can we eat breakfast first, Mr. Harrington?"

"It's Mike, Thomas. Let's eat and then go find your Victorian. You don't have an address, do you?"

Thomas shook his head as Sherrie arrived with her order pad and a cheery smile.

"Ready?" she asked.

They ordered. Thomas looked around the busy restaurant.

"You don't think he knows I'm in this hotel, do you?"

"This is a big city, but I think we need to be careful when we approach your new home."

Thomas shook his head. "I don't think of that old place as my home, Mr., uh, Mike."

"You probably wish you were back in Wyoming, working with the horses, don't you?"

"Well, yes. Part of me does. This trip is like riding a bronco in the rodeo. One minute it's a joyride, and the next, you're hitting the hard ground."

Their food arrived and the conversation stopped as they both dug in.

# Chapter 48

Mike took a sip of coffee. "The first thing we need to do when we get to the house is go up to your bedroom and get the will. That's going to tell us who's in line to inherent in the unlikely event of your death."

Thomas mopped yolk from his plate with his toast. He finished eating and pushed his plate away.

"How about the camera?"

"That's the second thing we'll do."

"Do you mind hanging out for a minute while I go up to my room and get my hat?"

"I'll be here drinking my coffee. Take your time."

When Thomas came back, he wore a western-cut suit, a dazzling silver belt buckle with inlaid coral, and new black boots, with red leather designs.

Mike whistled. "You look like a wealthy landowner. Nice threads. I hope you can walk in those boots. The car's on the back forty."

"Let's go. I wouldn't know how to walk in any other kind of footwear, Mike."

Mike pulled into traffic. "I know the vicinity of those Victorians, but Abdul wasn't specific about a house number. I don't suppose you know it."

"Gosh, no. It's blue . . . I was pretty dazzled when the cab pulled up."

"We'll find it, even if we need to knock on the door of every blue Victorian on the street."

When they came to the section of town known as Victorian Row, there was an ashy pall in the air.

"I have a bad feeling, Thomas."

Traffic crawled as they drove down the street.

"Looky-loos," Mike commented. The car in front of them stopped. Someone honked.

"Any of these houses look familiar?" Mike asked.

"No, I think it's after that curve up ahead."

Traffic started moving slowly. They could see a cop in the street, directing cars into the oncoming lane.

"This is crazy," Mike said. "I'm pulling into this driveway. Nobody's going to drive out of here anyway."

They got out of the car and walked toward the curve. Neighbors stood in their yards, looking at the smoke.

"Do you know which house it is?" Mike called to a couple, holding the leash of a basset hound.

"We think it is Madeline Sweet's house," the man answered. "Gone now. It's a shame."

Thomas ran ahead. When Mike came around the curve, he was talking with, who he assumed, was the butler. He watched as the firemen folded their hoses. Police put up yellow crime-scene tape to the singed shrubbery and a few lawn statues.

The butler wiped his face on a white handkerchief.

"Do you have someplace to go?" Thomas asked.

"My sister," he gurgled, amid fresh tears. He staggered off, holding the handkerchief to his face.

"Poor guy," Thomas said.

"How are you holding up?" Mike asked him.

"Oh, I'm sorry the old relic burned down, but I wasn't attached to it. Now, we don't have the will. A stricken look crossed his face. "Do you suppose the murderer did this to cover up my death?"

"That's exactly what I think."

They were quiet as they walked back to Mike's car.

"Thomas, do you remember the lawyer's name?" Mike asked as he backed out of the driveway.

"It was Banner. There were other names, but Mr. Banner read the will."

Michael stopped the car and pulled out his phone. He thumbed and then typed. Thomas looked on, curious.

"This must be it. Fitch, Banner and Adams. Does that sound right, Thomas?"

"I guess. Are you going to call him?"

"No. Let's visit him. I know this address . . ."

They were quiet as Mike drove until Thomas spoke.

"Are you thinking what I'm thinking, Mike?"

"You said you had a half-sister who was demonstrably upset at the reading of the will."

"That's right! She could have stabbed me and she could have set the house on fire . . . but Mike, could she carry me down the stairs and stuff me into the furnace?"

"No, you're right."

"But," Thomas said, "she could have promised the cook a few million to do the heavy work."

Mike remembered Ruby's description of the cook with his bloodied apron.

"Here we are. We'll know more after we see the will." He pulled into a parking place. After checking the directory, they took the elevator to the third floor.

"I'll do the talking, to get us in, and then you can take over. Okay?"

"Sure, Mike."

The door read, 'Fitch, Banner and Adams Attorneys at Law,' in gold leaf. They entered.

A young woman looked up from her computer. Mike glanced at the name on the Scrabble stand, spelled out in tiles —Monica Lawson.

"That must have been a triple-score, Monica."

She smiled.

"We're here to see Mr. Banner about the honor he's due for contributing all that equipment to the league. He knows about it," Mike said convincingly.

"Oh, he'll be thrilled. Go on in. I'll notify him."

They entered the office. Banner was on the phone, explaining how he'd filched a lucrative case from an attorney in a different group. He faced the window, his feet on the sill. Mike pointed to a multiple-switching device on the desk. One red light was on. He flipped the switch off.

Banner finally said, "Fred? Fred? Are you there? . . . Shit!"

He lowered his feet off the sill, turned, and slammed the receiver down. Mike and Thomas stood in front of his desk.

# Chapter 49

Banner's eyes rolled up, and he slid down onto the carpet behind his desk.

"What do I do now, Mike?" Thomas whispered.

"Push the intercom button labeled 'Secretary'. Tell her to bring the Madeline Sweet will. Try to sound like Banner."

Thomas's eyes got big, but he found the button on the box, pushed it, and after clearing his throat, spoke in his deepest voice.

"Right away, Mr. Banner."

"That was real smart, Mike," Thomas whispered.

The receptionist came in, carrying a folder. She wore her sandy hair in a bun. She reminded Thomas of one of his nicer foster mothers.

"I'll take that off your hands." He flashed a sincere smile. She looked into his friendly green eyes and let him take the file from her.

"Thank you, Miss . . .?"

"Cassidy. Pamela Cassidy. You're welcome. Mr. . . . .?"

"Call me Thomas, Pamela."

She blushed and pulled her beige cardigan tighter and then noticed her boss wasn't at his desk.

"Where . . .? Oh, Mr. Banner! What happened?" She dropped to the floor beside him.

"He just sagged down. Probably low blood sugar. Put your sweater under his head and fan him. There. He's already coming around."

Mike nudged Thomas toward the door.

"I'll be moseying along, Pamela. Tell Mr. Banner I said thanks," Thomas said.

In the car, they immersed themselves in the where-ases and parties-of-the-first-parts of the document.

"Here it is! Banner's motive!"

He read it to Mike.

"In the event, Thomas Cody, the primary beneficiary of Madeline Eloise Sweet's will, predeceases the disbursement of said benefits of the will, the benefits are to be disbursed to charities, to be chosen, and managed by executor, Raymond Cyril Banner, Attorney at Law, in perpetuity."

"We need to get to the police station," Mike said. "He's probably buying a plane ticket, right now."

He backed out of the parking space and drove the five blocks to the cop shop.

They hurried up the shallow steps. 'Denver Justice Center' was etched soberly in pale grey stone over the entrance. Thomas pushed the heavy glass door and they went in. A lone woman, sitting behind the glass shield, looked up. She wore cat's eyeglasses.

"We need to see the Chief of Police. It's important that we alert him to the fact that two serious attempts to murder Mr. Cody here were made, and the perpetrator is probably getting away as we speak."

She punched a few buttons and listened to her headset.

"An officer will escort you in. Please take a seat."

Finally, the door opened. A blue-uniformed officer came through. He led them down the hall to a scanner.

Put your keys and pocket contents on the tray, please," he instructed. "Step through here. One at a time, please."

Three turns down the grey hall and six doors later, he stopped. "Detective Inspector O'Malley's in here," he announced.

They hurried in and quickly explained the murder attempts by the attorney. Thomas handed over the will, folded to the incriminating clause.

"How do I know Banner tried to murder you?" asked O'Malley.

Thomas took off his suit coat and pulled up the shirt back to show the red, angry stab marks on his back.

"He was stuffed into the furnace of the Victorian house he was to inherit. Last night the house burned to the ground," Mike explained. The department surely knows about the arson job.

The detective barked instructions into his phone.

"Raymond Cyril Banner. Yeah. Now!"

O'Malley raked his hand through his red hair, as he hurried down the hall. Mike and Thomas followed.

"I'll have copies made of your document, Mr. Cody," Officer Willoughby said. He punched the keypad and opened the door to the foyer.

"They'll be returned in a moment. Have a seat," an officer told them. We're bringing Banner in for questioning."

They sat on hard chairs in the grey room which smelled like cleaning detergent.

"One more formality, Mr. Cody."

Thomas was escorted into an office, where he signed papers pressing charges.

"All done. Just stay in town."

As they walked toward the parking lot, a siren began to wail. A police car, emergency light flashing, sped by with Officer

Willoughby at the wheel and Chief Inspector O'Malley in the front passenger seat.

# Chapter 50

"That was pretty exciting, Mike, but now, I don't have an executor of the will."

"Hmm. You should consult someone outside of that firm, to represent you."

"Do you know an honest attorney, Mike?"

They walked to his car. "Actually, I don't know any attorneys, honest or otherwise. But I know someone who does. Do you have plans tonight?" he asked Thomas.

"Heck, no! I guess I'll go back to the hotel, lay around in my room, and watch TV."

"As I said, I'm the news anchor on Channel 7. I know the station can come up with a good attorney for you. Let's you and I go to my house, eat some lunch, and you can meet my fiancé. Sound like a plan?"

"Better than my plan," he said as he got into the car. "You sure your lady wants to meet an out-of-work, black cowboy from Wyoming?"

Mike grinned as he entered traffic. "I think she'll be delighted. You two should definitely meet."

They chatted as Mike drove through Denver.

"I don't remember Denver much," Thomas confessed. "I was just a kid in foster care going to different schools as I got shifted to the next home and new parents. I didn't know it was this large."

"Well, you won't *need* to live here after the lawsuit gets resolved. You worked on a horse ranch, right? Once you receive your inheritance, you could go back to Wyoming and buy your *own* horse ranch."

They pulled into Mike's driveway and into the garage.

"I hope Ruby's home. She's going to be surprised to see you, Thomas." They entered the service room. An aroma of cooking filled the air.

Ruby met them at the door to the kitchen with a large wooden spoon in her hand. Her hair was wound into a topknot. She wore jeans, a red flannel shirt, and one of Mike's aprons. Her eyes widened when she saw who was with him.

"Thomas! Wow! How are you?" she stuttered, clearly confused about how to talk to her saved victim.

"I'm doing pretty good, consider... uh, have we met before?" Thomas asked.

"Where are my manners? Come in. Thomas, my name is Ruby, and I have indeed met you but . . . well, sit at the counter. Let's tell each other everything."

They all had big smiles on their faces as Duchess and Duke trotted in. Duchess dropped a slobbery ball at Thomas's feet while Mike surveyed the drink selection in the refrigerator.

"Dr. Pepper or tea, Thomas?" Mike asked. "Or considering the past few days, maybe you'd like a beer."

"If you don't mind, I'd love a beer. My head's been in a spin since I got to Denver."

Mike served Thomas a bottle of Pacifico and poured iced tea for Ruby and himself.

Thomas took a long drink, while Ruby considered how much to tell this young man.

"You haven't heard the latest, Ruby," Mike said. "We set out to find the house this morning to get the will and check the camera. When we drove into the neighborhood, we realized there was a huge fire down the street. It was Thomas's house."

"Oh no! Was anyone in it?"

"The butler was standing in the front yard. He was distraught, but he was going to stay with his sister," Thomas told her. "I asked him about the cook. It was his day off. So we called on the attorney to get a copy of the will. When he saw me alive, he fainted. He would have benefited massively if I'd died. We took the will straight to the police station."

"And that brings me into the scenario, Thomas," Ruby said. "This might be hard to believe, but you're a recipient of my . . . um, ministrations as an amateur . . . Angel of Death."

Thomas cocked his head. "Uh, would you say that again, Miss Ruby?"

"Thomas, I won a Metaphysical Lottery, and this is the crazy part, the prize was to become anyone I wanted to for two weeks. I knew it wasn't real, as any intelligent person *would* know, so I chose to be the Angel of Death. But . . . it *was* granted. That's how I met you, as you lay dying in that furnace."

Thomas put down his beer, looked around the kitchen, and rubbed his eyes.

"So I'm dead?"

"You're very much alive, Thomas. You *were* dying in the furnace. That's why Abdul took me to you. I have discretion as the A.O.D. to let you die or to restore you to life. I granted you life."

Thomas looked like he didn't know whether to laugh or cry. Ruby put her arm around his shoulder and hugged him. He flinched.

"But . . . you look like an ordinary person!"

"I know this is a bit overwhelming on top of all you've been through, my friend, but Mike and I are here to help. And we *are* ordinary people."

"Actually," Mike said, "we're *hungry* ordinary people! I say we dish up this stew and eat."

Duke and Duchess, who knew the routine, banished themselves from the kitchen as the stranger and their humans began to eat.

# Chapter 51

Mike and Thomas left to go to the television station downtown. After cleaning the kitchen, Ruby called the dogs and took them into the backyard.

The day was blustery, blowing leaves off the scrub oak that had turned gold and red. As they air danced to the ground, Duchess and Duke thought it was great fun to leap for them.

Ruby walked the perimeter of the large yard, checking for snakes, but her mind was on a man she'd noticed the previous day as she and Abdul walked back to the cab after placing the camera in the cellar of the Victorian. He was across the street in the yard of a stately pale green home. He had caught her attention when he stepped behind a large tree as their eyes met.

Thinking back, she realized the man had *seen her in Angel mode.* In her mind's eye, something else was strange about it that she couldn't pin down, but it seemed important that she remember.

Suddenly, a sound penetrated her senses. She leaped back, adrenalin surging. The snake rattled on even as Ruby ran across the yard calling the dogs. "Treat time! The yard's all yours, Mr. Snake!"

Ruby's heart was still pounding as she pulled out the treat bag. Duke and Duchess happily danced around her.

"I just saved your lives, you turkeys." She gave each a twisted beef chew and drew a glass of water for herself. Her pink phone moaned taps, and the room reverberated with loud bangs of the door knocker.

"Oh, cra . . . kers! Coming, Abdul!"

By the time Ruby threw open the door, Abdul was sitting in the cab, looking composed. Buster was on his hind legs, head and front paws out the open back window, waiting for her to climb in.

"How do you do that Abdul?"

"And good afternoon to you too, Miss Ruby. How do I do what?"

She climbed into the back seat beside Buster. "Oh, never mind. Where are we off to today?"

"A long ride to the east side of town, Miss Ruby, close to the airport."

Ruby scratched Buster's neck, behind his ears.

"Don't do that," he complained.

"Why not? Don't you like it? My dogs love to be scratched behind their ears."

"Yeah, but they're just dogs. Plain, ordinary dogs."

"And you're not," Ruby said. "You're special."

"Well, duh!"

It was a long ride. Ruby sat back and thought about her close encounter with the rattlesnake. Too close. And then she remembered what her mind was concentrating on, instead of her usual vigilance.

"Abdul, did you see the man across the street from Madeline's yard yesterday when we put the camera in the cellar? We were walking back to the cab, and he stepped behind a tree."

"No, Miss Ruby. It sounds furtive. I'm usually aware of stranger activity in my immediate area." He paused and glanced at her in the rear-view mirror. "Do you know who he was?"

"That's the strange thing. My mind keeps going back to him . . . like I should know who he is, but I can't put my finger on it. The other strange thing, Abdul, is he looked into my eyes, and I was in Angel mode!"

"That's impossible, Miss Ruby. Unless he was dying, and then I would have known about him. You're right. It *is* strange."

Abdul turned into a side street that led into a subdivision. The developer had built three different house plans and as many paint colors. The streets curved, but the blocks marched on and on, mile after mile. Each street leading off the main street was named after a tree. Elm, Pine, and Oak. There were trees, but they were young ones that would take years to turn this somewhat bleak neighborhood into an inviting place. Ruby didn't see anybody out mowing grass, pushing a stroller, or pedaling a bicycle.

"Where is everybody?" she asked Abdul.

"Adults at work, kids in school, and babies in daycare, I presume. We're going to a shooting in progress, Miss Ruby."

"Yuck!" was her comment. Abdul navigated down street after similar street and pulled into the driveway of a beige house with chocolate brown shutters. As she opened the car door, they heard two shots from inside. Ruby and Buster rushed in.

The living room was empty, so they ran down the hall to what Ruby guessed, was the parent's bedroom. They found two boys. They were young, about twelve or thirteen, she thought. One was on the floor, spurting blood from his side. His face was drained of color, leaving his large map of freckles as red as his hair. The other boy, a caramel-skinned African American, stood, holding a pistol at his side. The horrified look on his face told Ruby the story.

"Put the gun on the floor," she said. He did and she was surprised that he could hear her.

253

"Get me a large clean towel from the bathroom. Quickly!"

She knelt beside the injured boy. While the other boy was in the bathroom, she waved her hand over the wounded child and felt the life-giving snap. The bleeding slowed to a dribble. Ruby stood and put the gun in the top drawer of the dresser.

"Hurry with that towel!" she yelled. "I think he's slipping away!"

Buster cocked his head at Ruby. The boy ran in with the towel, shoved it to Ruby, and stood back, too horrified to look at his friend.

"Kneel here and press the towel to the wound! Quickly! If you hear a death rattle, give him mouth-to-mouth! You know how to do that, don't you?" She said it in a rapid, near-panicked tone, so the boy would feel the horror of what he had done.

"I'll call the ambulance! You pray! Pray hard that your friend doesn't die!"

In the kitchen, after calling the ambulance, Ruby found a rolodex. Under D, she found the daycare number. She ran back to the boys. "What's your name?" she demanded.

"Pete," he said.

"Pete what?"

"Matheson," he whispered. "Is he going to d-die? I didn't ma-mean to shoot him. I didn't mean to pull the t-trigger!"

"Just keep pressing the towel to the wound and pray, like I told you."

"Do you have a child there with the last name of Matheson?" she asked the lady who answered. She checked and admitted that she did.

"Please call the mother of that child, and tell her there's been an accident at her home involving her son, Pete. Please tell her that everything is under control, but she absolutely needs to come home now. Will you do that?"

"Shall I tell her who called?"

"If she asks, just tell her it was an Angel." Ruby hung up, and she and Buster quietly slipped out the door.

In the taxi, Ruby noticed the knee of her jeans was soaked in blood. She sighed.

"Abdul, why could that boy see me? He wasn't dying."

"How old would you say he was?"

I'm guessing he was twelve or thirteen. Hard for me to know, but they were both young."

"Different rules for children. They're able to accept things that adults can't."

# Chapter 52

Abdul drove through the maze of streets while Ruby gazed out the window, her mind on the two unfortunate boys. She felt glad that she was the Angel who saved the boy, and, hopefully, taught Pete that guns weren't toys.

"Abdul! Stop!" she yelled. "I just saw him!"

Abdul stopped the cab. "Who? Where?"

"The man. The same man I saw across the street from Thomas's Victorian. He stepped out from the corner of that yellow house back there."

Ruby opened the car door and ran across the street. Abdul climbed out. "Ruby, wait!"

Buster ran after her, barking. Ruby arrived at the corner of the house, but the man was no longer there. She walked quietly along the side and peeked around the corner into the backyard. A large dog lunged against the fence, barking loudly. Buster growled. The fenced dog ran to the back porch.

"The man's gone, Buster. Let's go back to the cab. Thanks for dealing with the dog. That was impressive."

Buster pranced ahead. "No big deal," he growled.

Abdul stood beside the cab. "You should have waited for me to go with you, Miss Ruby. He could have been dangerous."

"I'm sorry, Abdul. Next time I see him, I'll wait. He just disappeared into thin air. Did you see him?"

"No, Miss Ruby. I looked . . . this is twice that you've seen a man and I didn't. Something strange is going on."

"Your eyes were on the road when he ducked around the corner of the house and then, poof! He was gone."

"You're certain it was the same man you saw before?"

"Yes. I have the feeling that I've seen him before all this started. I just can't place where."

Abdul drove back across the north side of Denver to Ruby and Mike's home. He pulled up to the door and stopped. "I'll do some checking, Miss Ruby."

The house was quiet. Duke and Duchess were sprawled on the rug in the great room, napping. Ruby made herself a cup of tea and curled up on the sofa with a book she hadn't had time to get past the first chapter. The room was warm. She fell asleep, snuggled against throw pillows.

She woke from a dream and sat up. "It's him!" she said out loud. Duke looked up from his own dream.

"Who?" he said in his Duke voice.

"You don't know him, Duke. A man from my first Angel of Death encounter." Ruby shivered. "Oh, wow. That's creepy . . . !"

Ruby looked out the big picture window she and Mike watched the sunset through in the evenings.

"What are you doing?" Duchess asked as Ruby crawled across the room and drew the drapes closed.

"There might be a man lurking around the house. I'd like for you two to keep vigilant and warn me if you see, smell, or hear anything. Okay?"

"Okay," they both said. "What's vigilant?"

Ruby smiled. "It just means keep listening."

Both dogs stood now and listened. "We don't hear anything," Duke growled.

"Good! That's what I want. Who wants dinner?"

Both dogs ran to the service room where their empty food bowls sat. Ruby locked the front door and followed them.

*Why would that man . . . I didn't . . . I'm sure he died . . . he was bleeding out when I left . . . maybe he died, and that's his . . . no . . . don't be silly. No such thing as . . . are there?*

Ruby picked up the two large dog bowls and scooped kibble into each one. She pulled a barely-cooked hamburger from the refrigerator and crumbled it into the dishes. The dogs sat patiently until she put the food down. She said, "Okay!" They scrambled to their dishes and wolfed the food. It made her smile.

The late afternoon sun that usually streamed through the window on the west side of the house was now blocked by the heavy drapes. Ruby always enjoyed the feel and look of the warm light filling the room.

"What am I afraid of?" she scoffed. "I'm the Angel of Death, and that means . . . " She drew back the drapes. *Does that protect me from angry . . . um, ghosts?* She remembered the pages of information she was supposed to read and hadn't. She wondered where she'd stashed them.

Ruby started down the hall to the room she'd moved into as an ex-Angel to save Michael from himself. Possibly the pages were still there.

The phone rang—it was the regular phone.

"Hi, Honey," Mike said. "After the news tonight, I'm going to take Thomas to meet an attorney. He knows a friend who has a car for sale. We'll go look at it. Maybe get him some wheels. We'll grab a bite here in town so don't cook dinner. Okay, Love?"

"No problem, Mike. If I need to leave, I'll write a note. Love you."

In the bedroom, she opened drawers of her undies, socks, and scarves, and in the bottom drawer, a plethora of bits and pieces of her former life, but no typed pages.

The closet shelves displayed shoes, hats, and sweaters, and when she reached up to the very top one, she found the papers.

"Voila!"

Ruby propped the pillows against the headboard, sat on the bed, and started to read. Duke and Duchess, who weren't allowed on other furniture in the house, remembered being on this bed when Ruby first moved in. They happily jumped up and collapsed, keeping her company.

RULES AND REGULATIONS, she read.

Article 1: Angel must, at all times, conduct herself in a timely and----bla------bla-----bla----!

Article 2: Bla----bla------------ must be accompanied at each encounter by her assistant, Buster, -------------------bla----bla----bla-----------------------------------------!

Ruby plowed on. This is just so much dribble, she thought as she read on. And on. Finally, she reached the last page.

"Nothing!" she pronounced. "Nothing about any protection from disgruntled dead people or *not* dead people I've encountered as the Angel of Death!"

Duchess tipped her head and watched Ruby toss the pages down.

# Chapter 53

"The wizard! That's who I need to ask." Ruby fished her pink phone from the back pocket of her jeans. She looked under W for wizard. *Not there.*

*What did he say to look under . . . some ancient music guy. Tchaikovsky? No, that doesn't sound right. Um . . . Mozart! Yes!*

Ruby punched in the number, 999-999-9999. *Hmmm. Strange number.* The "Marriage of Figaro" was the ringtone. She wondered how she knew that not being a classical music buff. It played on and on. *Do I really need to listen to the entire overture? Typical of the wizard, boring old fart.*

"HELLO, YES? YES? SPEAK UP, DEAR GIRL. I'M A VERY *BUSY,* BORING OLD FART, YOU KNOW!"

Ruby was so startled at his loud proclamation that she dropped the phone.

Recovering it, she said, "Sorry about the boring old fart thing, Mr. Wizard. I . . . I have a very puzzling situation happening. You're the only one who can answer my question.

"YES, YES! ASK YOUR QUESTION, DEAR GIRL! WHAT IS IT?"

"Well, Mr. Wizard, my very first Angel of Death call involved a young woman and an older, rather scrofulous man. I saved the woman and left the man to die. Now, I see him lurking when I'm on call and he instantly disappears when I try to confront him. Is he a ghost or is he alive? And, more importantly, am I in danger?"

"IS HE DRESSED THE SAME AS WHEN YOU SAW HIM ALIVE, OR HAS HE CHANGED CLOTHES?"

"Hmm. I don't remember noticing how he was dressed on either the first occasion or the latest sightings. Do you think it's important?"

"WELL, YES. IF HE'S IN THE SAME CLOTHES AS YOUR FIRST ENCOUNTER, THEN HE'S A GHOST ... OR, PERHAPS HE JUST HAS A VERY LIMITED WARDROBE."

"Well, excuse me for saying, Mr. Wizard, but that's not very helpful. Don't you have some wizardly powers that you can research this person? And can't you tell me if I have Angel immunity from disgruntled, uh, fatalities in which I might have been involved?

"UM, LET ME CHECK ... " Ruby heard pages fluttering. "MUMBLE, MUMBLE, NO NOT THAT ... MAYBE ... NO." Flutter, flutter. "AHA! ... NO. NEVER MIND. UH, MY DEAR, ARE YOU STILL THERE?"

"Still here, Mr. Wizard."

"MY DEAR, DO YOU HAPPEN TO KNOW THIS PERSON'S NAME? THAT MIGHT HELP MY SEARCH."

"When I asked him his name, he said it was Daffy Duck. I addressed him as Mr. Duck, but I'm positive it was an alias. Surely, Mrs. Duck wouldn't name her baby son, Daffy. You could ask Abdul if he knows the man's name."

"ABDUL? WHO IS THIS ABDUL?"

"You know who Abdul is. He's the man you assigned to drive the cab and take me to my Angel calls."

"NO! THE MAN I ASSIGNED TO DRIVE YOU TO YOUR CALLS IS PETER PETERS. IT SAYS SO RIGHT HERE."

"Look, Mr. Wizard! This isn't solving my problem. Abdul is my helper and my driver no matter what your page says. I've never met this Peter Peters person. May we get back to my original question, please?"

"AH . . . LOOK, I'LL DO SOME RESEARCH AND CALL YOU BACK. YOU'LL KNOW MY RINGTONE."

And that said, the wizard hung up.

*Well, that wasn't very helpful . . . but it did remind me that I've only seen Daffy Duck on A.O.D. calls. That's comforting.*

Ruby slid off the bed, and the dogs followed. "Nothing to be afraid of here, my curly friends. Let's go out to the yard and play."

Duchess and Duke romped all the way to the back door. She remembered the snake incident and told them to sit on the deck while she walked the fence and scanned the yard.

"All clear!" No snake and no ghost, she noted, with an easy heart.

They played until the sun dipped below the mountaintop in the west and the ball she'd been throwing was so slobbery that Ruby cringed each time she picked it up.

# Chapter 54

Ruby microwaved a large bowl of left-over stew, and after a longing look at the beer in the refrigerator, drew a glass of water and sat at the bar to eat.

Nine months is a long time, and I'm barely into it. I need to order a book about pregnancy and keep track of Baby Harrington's progress. She sighed. Still hungry. *Remember, eating for two now.* She dished herself a generous bowl of strawberry chocolate fudge ice cream. She sat on the sofa, slowly ate the treat, and watched the sunset. Slipping her shoes off, she curled up and reached for the remote control to turn on the six o'clock news, curious if Mike would talk about Thomas Cody's odyssey.

The pink phone chimed, loudly. The door knocker reverberated through the entire house. Ruby slipped on her shoes and ran to the door. As usual, Abdul was already seated behind the wheel of his scruffy, yellow taxi.

"Wait one minute, Abdul, while I grab a jacket." She quickly scribbled a note to Mike and came out, pulling on her jeans jacket.

"Where to, and by the way, do you know a Peter Peters?"

"Good evening, Miss Ruby. How are you, this evening?"

"I'm just fine, my friend, How are you? And do you know a Peter Peters?"

There was a long pause. Ruby checked Abdul's expression in the rear-view mirror. As usual, there was no change, but his eyes glanced to the mirror and noted Ruby watching him. Buster, on the seat beside her, watched, too.

"You have spoken to the wizard."

"Yes, I wanted to know if he knew who the mysterious man is. I need to know if he's alive or a ghost and if he can hurt me."

"What did the wizard tell you?"

"He asked me the man's name. Remember the man in the Cinna-Bun shooting? I realized that's the man I keep seeing. He told me his name was Daffy Duck. I told the wizard to ask you, but he doesn't know who you are . . . he thinks my driver is named Pe—"

Abdul interrupted. "We're here, Miss Ruby. There's about to be a serious wreck. We'll continue this conversation, afterward."

Ruby looked around. They were on the street leading to the apartment she lived in before. A scream of brakes and the ugly sound of metal slamming into metal, and then, hideous screeching.

*This is like déjà vu. The very reason I chose to be the Angel of Death.* When she opened her eyes, she saw the car, torn apart, emitting steam and leaking fluids, masses of unrecognizable metal, and other large chunks. A large truck had spun to the side of the street, relatively undamaged.

"I need to get the people out of the wreck, Abdul!" She climbed out of the cab, Buster, right behind her.

The sirens were loud, telling Ruby they were almost here. She knew they couldn't see her or Buster, so she held back. A fire truck pulled in, behind two cop cars, lights flashing and sirens, dying. The ambulance siren was still about a block away, but coming fast.

Miraculously, a man in a suit and a small boy were being pulled from the side of the car, seemingly only scraped and banged up.

*I know how this goes; I need to get to the woman.* Ruby panicked at the vision of the woman covered in a sheet and the man and the little boy sitting on the curb crying. It was seared into her memory.

Dodging between EMTs and the police, Ruby and Buster ran to the smashed-in side of the small sedan. The jaws of life were being hauled to the scene. Ruby had only seconds to reach through the shattered window of the mangled door and circle her hand over the inert body of the terribly injured woman. She wasn't certain if she'd gotten there in time. The men with the device ran to the side of the car. Ruby and Buster leaped away. They watched the jaws snap the metal in two as if it was a soda cracker. The cutters ripped the door apart and the EMT reached in.

"She's alive!" he shouted. The jaws cut through the seat mechanism, and the seat holding the injured woman was lifted out. Two big men carried her to the waiting ambulance.

Tears ran down Ruby's face. She and Buster walked back to the cab. Abdul stood, holding the door open for her as he always did. She felt slightly dazed. She climbed in.

"Abdul," she said in a husky voice, "I've already seen this *very* wreck happen *before* I became an Angel. The woman died. I was on the bus . . . Oh! There's the bus!"

Ruby was quiet, watching the bus go by. It stopped in the next block to let out a woman dressed in khaki slacks and a brown, knit shirt.

"I just saw the woman I was get off that bus! Why and *how* has this happened again, Abdul? Are we experiencing a wrinkle in time?"

Abdul pulled away from the curb. "You saw all this happen before you were the Angel of Death?"

"Yes."

"Had you won the Metaphysical Lottery when you saw this?"

"Um, now that I think about it, I went to the movie on Sunday, the day before the wreck. It happened the day after I won . . . that's significant, isn't it?"

"I think seeing the wreck was the first part of your metaphysical experience. It didn't really happen that day, Miss Ruby. It happened today when you were able to save that woman's life."

Ruby was quiet. *It makes some kind of sense but also seems rather manipulative . . . on the other hand, now I can put that terrible memory of the crying husband and child away and be glad I could change the outcome . . . but, that's why I chose to be the Angel of Death, because of the . . . fake wreck.*

"Abdul, can we discuss that other stuff, next time? I'm exhausted, confused, and all I can think of is a warm bath and bed."

# Chapter 55

*Mike's not home from helping Thomas deal with finding an attorney and . . . what else did he say? Too tired to care right now.*

She said hello to the dogs and stumbled into the large bathroom, remembered it was all shower, and dragged herself to the tub in her former bedroom.

*Yes! A nice big, deep bathtub.* While it filled, she shed her clothes, twisted her hair into a bun, pinned it, and climbed in.

"Ahhh . . . " Ruby closed her eyes and took a deep breath, letting it out with a sigh.

*Don't think about anything . . . don't think about anything . . . don't think a-b o u t . . .* Ruby slipped under the water . . . sublimely submerged, sliding into s l e e . . . .

She heard loud, insistent barking. Ruby sat up, pulling herself awake. Her eyes flew open. She took a huge breath, coughed, and looked around.

"Duchess! You saved my life! How did you know to bark and wake me? You're my savior."

"I told her to," Duke chimed in.

"You did not!" Duchess said. "You were busy licking your . . . "

"Never mind," Ruby said. "Move off my rug, please. I'm getting out."

When Mike got home, he found Ruby, Duke, and Duchess asleep in the guest bedroom.

Mike sat on the edge of the bed and kissed Ruby on the lips. Her eyes flew open.

"Mike! I—" She swung her legs to the floor and ran to the bathroom. Mike followed and found her on her knees in front of the commode.

"Ruby, are you alright?"

"I'm, I'm," and she vomited.

"Ruby, are you sick? What happened?"

She slowly stood, flushed the toilet, took a deep breath, and walked to the sink, where she rinsed her mouth.

"I'm pregnant, Mike, and it seems to have caught up with me. I hoped I would miss this unlovely development. I've read up. By the third month, this is usually over."

Mike put his arm around Ruby and led her to the bed. "Are you hungry? I can heat up some soup. And crackers! Have you eaten? Do you want to lie down? Or ice cream! Shall I get a cloth for your forehead?"

Ruby giggled. "Oh Mike, you're so cute. Thank you for being you. I'm very okay. According to conventional wisdom, this is a normal thing and not a bit dangerous or concerning other than the fact that it's not much fun. I'm just glad it didn't happen while I was . . . oh-oh."

"What, Ruby? Are you thinking what I'm thinking?"

"Mike, I need to call the wizard. I can't be an Angel of Death who vomits. Oh, Mike," she wailed.

"What, Ruby? Oh, you're crying." He wrapped his arms around her.

"It's okay," he murmured. "Tell me, Hon. Tell me why you're sad," he whispered.

"I don't know!" she sobbed.

Mike held her. "Is it about not being an Angel anymore?"

"Y-e, y-e-s. I just . . . saved a young boy from . . . dying. It was . . . so important, Mike. And then, a mom, in a terrible wreck! And now, I won't . . . " She sobbed, finally catching her breath. "Now, I'll just be an, an ordinary . . . "

"Ruby, my darling, you don't seem to realize that as a woman, you are the most important, powerful, amazing life form on this planet! Think about it. At this very moment, you are creating a brand-new human in your body, cell by cell, perfect in every way. And Ruby, in time, and this is mind-blowing, you will, all by yourself, actually give *birth* to this five-to-seven-pound baby, like it's no big deal!"

When Ruby looked at him, Mike had tears in his eyes and on his cheeks.

"And you'll be a MOTHER!" he continued. "Talk about important! Ruby, there wouldn't be a world without mothers. It's a lifetime job and not every woman gets to have this experience."

Ruby and Mike lay looking into each other's tear-filled eyes. Ruby smiled.

"Mike," she said.

"Yeah?" he said.

"I'm hungry again. Let's go feed this brand-new human."

# Epilogue

So that's how I, the former Ruby Louise Holliday, ended my metaphysical career as an Amateur Angel. As the Angel of Death, I allowed a few souls to live, and a few souls to die and ascend to Heaven which my beloved fiancé, Michael Harrington and I unclogged in order to welcome *all* souls to that lovely, restful, Heavenly vacation we all deserve after completing this complicated, exhausting life.

P.S. If you see a man who calls himself Daffy Duck, tell him it's time to go to Heaven.

Thank you for reading my story.
Yours *Very* Truly,
**Ruby Louise Harrington**